#1

Fire in the North

THE MITCHELL BROTHERS SERIES

Fire in the North

#1

THE MITCHELL BROTHERS SERIES

Brian McFarlane

Fenn Publishing Company Ltd.
Bolton, Canada

FIRE IN THE NORTH
BOOK ONE IN THE MITCHELL BROTHERS SERIES
A Fenn Publishing Book

Fenn Publishing Company Ltd.
Bolton, Ontario, Canada

Distributed in Canada by H. B. Fenn and Company Ltd.
Bolton, Ontario, Canada, L7E 1W2
www.hbfenn.com

National Library of Canada Cataloguing in Publication

McFarlane, Brian, 1931-
        Fire in the north / Brian McFarlane.

(Mitchell brother series ; 1)
ISBN 1-55168-243-5

        I. Title. II. Series.

PS8575.F37F47 2003   jC813'.54   C2003-902103-3
PZ7

FIRE IN THE NORTH

Brian McFarlane, with 53 books to his credit, is one of Canada's most prolific authors of hockey books. He comes by his writing honestly, for he is the son of Leslie McFarlane, a.k.a. Franklin W. Dixon, author of the first 21 books in the Hardy Boys series. With his father in mind and with two brothers not unlike the Hardy Boys as his central characters, Brian has written *Fire in the North*, a story based on the great fire that destroyed the McFarlane homestead and practically all of the town of Haileybury, Ontario many years ago.

NOTE FROM THE AUTHOR

Many years ago, a raging forest fire swept through my father's hometown of Haileybury, destroying everything in its path, including my grandfather's house, and resulting in much loss of life.

My father, Leslie McFarlane, then a young reporter living in Sudbury, would write about the tragedy on the front pages of the *Sudbury Star*. Even as he wrote, he did not know whether or not his parents and three brothers had survived the total destruction of his hometown.

With my father in mind, I bring you the first book in the Mitchell Brothers Series, *Fire in the North*.

Brian McFarlane

CHAPTER 1

A TRIP TO THE FIRE TOWER

On the outskirts of the town of Haileybury, brothers Max and Marty Mitchell rode their bicycles along a dusty, deserted road. It was a September morning in 1935 and already the boys were drenched in sweat. It was the hottest fall day either could remember.

"We're almost there!" shouted Max to his younger brother. He took one hand off the handlebars, whipped off his cap and stuffed it in his back pocket. He ran a hand through his thick blond hair, then turned to check on his brother Marty, who was riding close behind him. "Another half-mile, Marty. You're a little red in the face. You getting tired?"

"No, no, I'm fine," Marty lied. He was breathing hard and his legs were beginning to wobble on the pedals. Marty was two years younger and two inches shorter than Max, who was 16. The last couple of miles, Marty had been forced to pedal harder than his brother—fighting to keep up. The gap between

1

the bicycles widened. Max was a born athlete, Marty thought enviously. Almost six feet tall already, with broad shoulders and a slim waist. No wonder he was so popular at school. The girls loved his blue eyes and his ready smile. Marty wiped the sweat from his brow with one hand. The bike wobbled. His legs felt like spaghetti noodles. "Max, there's a small brook up ahead. Let's stop and get a drink."

They swept down a hill and skidded to a stop on the sandy bank of a small, fast stream that tumbled over rocks and disappeared into a culvert under the road. The boys jumped off their bikes and ran to the water. They drank until their sides hurt.

"Now I feel better," Marty said, splashing water on his face and over his shock of red-brown hair.

"You trying to wash the red out?" Max asked Marty.

Marty chuckled and squirted a jet stream of water out of his mouth and caught Max square in the face.

"Jeez!" Max howled. "I was only kidding."

Marty flopped back on a patch of dry grass. "I can't believe it's so hot. At this rate it will never cool down for the hockey season."

"Don't you worry about that, little brother. The ice in the lake will be three feet thick before you know it." He walked toward some trees.

"Hey, Max, what are you doing? Where you going?" Marty raised himself to one elbow.

"I've got to see a man about a dog, is all."

"A dog. There's no dog in there. What dog?" Marty leaped to his feet.

There was no answer. When Max emerged from behind the tree he was doing up the buttons on his fly. He grinned at his brother.

"It's just an expression, Marty," he explained. "It means a guy has to take a leak. Get it?"

"Yeah, I get it," Marty said, grinning.

Max picked up his bike. "You ready? Let's go."

"Wait a sec, willya?" Marty replied, laughing. He darted into the woods. "I've got to see if that man with the dog is still around."

In a few moments the brothers, relieved and refreshed, were on their way again, with Max setting a fast pace.

"One more hill and we'll be at the fire tower," Max said, breathing hard despite the fact he was in excellent shape. Hockey season would soon be starting and he wanted to be the best-conditioned player on the team.

"Let's go then, brother," Marty replied, pumping hard on his bike and passing Max. He took a lead of about ten yards before shouting back over his shoulder, "I'll race you to the tower."

Max laughed and took up the chase. Gradually he began to overtake Marty, who was now halfway up the hill and laughing with excitement. "Be careful Marty!" Max called out. "You're wandering into the centre of the road." But Marty didn't hear. He was pumping hard now, and grunting through clenched teeth. He was a competitor, determined to win the race. Marty put his head down and pedalled harder. Suddenly the boys heard the roar of an engine. A car crested the hill and bounced toward them, a big yellow Buick travelling at tremendous speed, almost out of control. "Marty, look out!" Max screamed, twisting his handlebars and swerving to the right, trying to get out of the way. His brother, closer to the brink of the hill and swaying from side to side from his exertions, was in more immediate danger. Instinctively, Marty turned away from the oncoming car, held up one hand as if to ward off the vehicle and leaped from the bike. He flew through the air and tumbled to the ground, rolling over and over to avoid the spinning wheels, which threw loose dirt and small pebbles in all directions. The fender of the car missed Marty's legs by inches. Max fell right behind his brother, heard the roar of the engine as one fender of the car brushed his body and felt the breath whoosh out of him when he hit the gravel— hard. The brothers lay in shock by the side of the road, fighting for breath and blinded by a cloud of dust kicked up by the vehicle that had almost taken their lives.

"That idiot!" Marty gasped, rubbing dust from his eyes. "He almost ran right over us."

Max jumped to his feet. "You're right. He's insane to drive like that. Look! He's stopping at the bottom of the hill."

The Buick had come to a skidding halt. Through the dust the boys could see a large man step out of the car. He wore a wide-brimmed straw hat, a plaid shirt, red suspenders and heavy work boots. The man glared at the Mitchell boys. Deliberately, he spit a stream of chewing tobacco to the ground. He raised a thick arm and made a fist. "Stupid kids!" he shouted. "Hogging the road like that. You're lucky I didn't squash you!"

Max was speechless. He thought the driver might be concerned that he'd almost killed two kids on bikes. He might begin by saying he was sorry. Why wasn't he running up the hill to find out if anyone had been seriously injured? Max began to realize there would be no apology, no remorse, and no show of regret. The stranger continued to stand there, fist upraised. He was furious. He was blaming them!

Max cupped one hand to his mouth and shouted back. "You were in the wrong, mister! Not us. You were speeding and driving recklessly. You almost killed us. If you had you'd be charged with manslaughter."

"Oh, yeah, well who'd be left to charge me? You two little squirts would be flatter than pancakes on a platter. And you're a mouthy pair. I have half a mind to come up there and give you both a good licking." His hands went to his wide leather belt. He took a couple of steps toward them. Marty grabbed his brother by the sleeve. He whispered, "Max, let's get ready to run for it."

Max said, "Quiet, Marty. Not yet." He bent down and picked up a fair-sized rock. "Half a mind is about all you've got, mister," he said. "Come on up. You've got your belt and I've got this rock," Max said. "That makes it an even fight, I'd say." His hands were steady; his voice betrayed no fear.

The man hesitated. The kid he'd almost killed a minute ago, a cocky teenager, was now challenging him to back up his tough talk. The kid wasn't intimidated. And he handled that rock like he knew how to throw it. And there were more rocks where that one came from. Once again, the stranger spit into the dirt. Then he snarled, "I'll let you two punks off this time because I've got to get to town. Got to meet the boat and I'm late. Next time, stay out of my way." He jumped in the car, put the vehicle in gear and started to drive away.

"Can you see his licence number, Max?" Marty asked.

"Not from this distance. Too much dust. Looks like it begins with PU. Can't see the rest of it."

"PU. That licence suits a stinker like him," Marty said. His face brightened. "Hey, brother," he said,

6

"that was some show you put on. With the rock and all. You made him think twice about coming after us. You made him back right down. Good going, Max."

"If you stand up to a bully, he'll often show his true colours," said Max. "I learned that on the hockey rink."

"But what if he had come after us. He had arms like a gorilla. What would you have done then, Max?"

"I'd have done what any kid would have done." Max laughed out loud. "I'd have thrown the rock and then run through the woods like a scared rabbit."

CHAPTER 2
A RANGER'S LONELY LIFE

The fire tower was a tall wooden structure built deep in the woods, high on a hill. From a small room at the top of the tower, a forest ranger could see for miles. In every direction there were rolling hills, shimmering lakes and a forest that stretched all the way to the hazy horizon.

The ranger on duty this day was a tall, dark-haired, good-natured man named William "Billy" Mitchell. At dawn each morning from spring until fall, Ranger Mitchell, his lunch bucket and his binoculars slung over his back, climbed up a long ladder attached to one side of the tower until he reached a small door that opened into his lonely perch. Once inside his workstation, shaded by a roof that protected him from sun and rain but not annoying blackflies and mosquitoes, he began his monotonous vigil, which consisted of a dawn to dusk scrutiny of the miles of forest that stretched out all around him.

Using powerful binoculars, he scanned the countless square miles of treetops. In hot, dry weather, any sign of smoke caught his keen eye. He knew a small fire could be whipped by winds into a raging fireball, awesome and deadly. North Country people knew the danger. Many had learned from painful experience that a runaway bushfire could wipe out any community in its path.

Ranger Mitchell looked at his watch. Visitors were due any minute. His nephews Max and Marty, his brother Harry's sons, had promised to bicycle out from Haileybury.

Max wanted to interview his uncle about a day in the life of a forest ranger. He aspired to be a writer and he was hoping his father, the owner and editor of the *Haileyburian*, would print his story. Marty rode with him simply because he insisted on going everywhere that Max went. Well, almost everywhere. In town there was a girl named Sally Logan who also enjoyed being with Max. Her face lit up whenever he came around. But if Marty was tagging along, her smile became forced; her eyes lost their sparkle. Marty was amused at her discomfort. He knew what she was thinking. *Not you again, little brother. Can't you find someone your own age to play with?*

"Hello up there! Uncle Bill!"

The ranger leaned over the railing of his perch—

he called it his "office"—and saw two grinning faces far below.

"C'mon up!" he shouted.

The boys scrambled up the ladder. He gave them each a hug.

They looked like they'd come through a dust storm! Or a cement mixer.

"We had a close call on the road. A crazy driver almost ran us down," Marty said.

"That's serious stuff, boys," Ranger Mitchell said. "Tell me about it. Looks like you survived, even though your clothes have been through the mill."

Marty described the incident on the hill and how the stranger had almost bowled them over. The ranger examined his nephews for cuts and bruises and patched up a few minor scrapes. Then he turned to Max and grinned. "So you want to make me famous, do you? Put my name in all the papers? Write a story about the glamorous life of a fire ranger? Sell the movie rights? Make me a star like Al Jolson or Douglas Fairbanks? Is that what we're doing today?"

Max laughed. He pulled a notebook out of his backpack and went fishing for a pencil. "No, Uncle Bill, I'm doing a story about the life of a forest ranger for Dad's paper. If it's any good he'll even pay me for it."

Uncle Bill winked at Marty. "How can it not be

good if it's all about me? Why didn't we conduct this interview in my new home in Cobalt? Small as it may be, devoid of indoor plumbing as it is, with floors that squeak and a roof that leaks, it's still a palace to me."

"Wouldn't be the same, Uncle Bill. A good reporter always goes to the scene of the story. You know, to capture the atmosphere. That's what Dad says, anyway. So we'll visit you in your palace another time, when we're properly dressed for it."

Marty waved a box camera in the air—one of the new Kodaks. "We borrowed Dad's camera to get some shots of you at work, Uncle Bill. He said he'd put them in the paper if they turn out."

"Got it," said their uncle. "Click away, Marty. I have no bad sides. And a great profile. Say, I brought an extra thermos of lemonade, boys. And your Aunt Elsie made some peanut butter cookies for us. So let's have a snack, then you can ask me any questions you want."

While they sipped the cool lemonade and munched on the cookies, the boys took a moment to enjoy the view.

"Wow!" exclaimed Marty. "You can see the whole world from up here."

"Not quite," chuckled the ranger.

"Well, most of the North Country then," Marty said, shading his eyes with one hand.

"A good portion of it," said their uncle. "But there are still hundreds of square miles of bush country you can't see from this tower. I'd hate to see a forest fire destroy a single acre of it."

Max was beginning to take notes.

"I know they have forest fires in other places, too, Uncle Bill—like Texas or California." he said.

"Oh, sure they do. Anywhere there's a forest there's always a chance a bolt of lightning will burn some of it down. Or some fool who doesn't know how to put out his campfire or tosses a cigarette butt away will start a blaze. That kind of recklessness sickens me."

The pencil in Max's hand flew over the page.

"I imagine others envy us our great forests," added the forest ranger. "But I don't know how they'd survive in them. I'd love to see someone who lives on the prairie try to wade through the northern bush."

Uncle Bill chuckled, sat back in his chair and pushed his broad-brimmed ranger hat back on his head. "He'd be chased by bears and wolves and sprayed by skunks. He'd be forced to swim rapids and climb rocky outcroppings. He'd step in holes he wouldn't see and poison ivy he wouldn't recognize. He'd sweat through his clothes under the noonday sun and by midnight he'd be a shivering mess, so cold he'd break out in goose bumps big as billiard balls and he'd swear the blood in his veins had turned to slush. And there'd be no one around to sympathize with him; no one who'd care two hoots about his complaints—or his survival. He'd be..."

"Wait a sec, Uncle Bill. I can't write fast enough to keep up with you." Max was scribbling furiously. "Okay," he said, "you were saying?"

Max continued to take notes, although his hand was getting tired. "Give me another minute, Uncle Bill."

"Sure, son, and while you're catching up I'll do a bit of work up here. You know this is my last week on the job. Season's almost over. All the fire stations close down at the end of the week."

"But why?" Max asked.

"The government feels most of the danger of fires is over by October. And it usually is. But this year is the exception. Closing the fire towers now is just plain stupid. Look over there! See all that haze to the north? There are some big fires burning because it's been so hot and dry. And a couple of smaller ones I spotted close to Haileybury. There are lots of men out fighting them. But the danger won't be over until we get a good downpour or a foot of snow. Government's closing us down anyway."

He raised his binoculars and began a sweep of the horizon. Then he made several more sweeps, each time covering an area of bushland that brought him closer to the tower. He explained to his nephews what he was doing and how he did it.

"I check the whole area every half-hour or so," he said. "Takes me about ten minutes to do a thorough job. By nightfall my poor eyes are red and sore from staring through these glasses most of the day. Want to try it, lads?"

Both boys were thrilled to peer through the glasses. They were amazed at what they saw. Tall jack pines, black spruce, golden patches of brush bordering an isolated lake of cobalt blue. Multi-coloured maples and granite rocks in hues of brown and gray. And when they turned the glasses to the north, the images blurred because of the dense haze that rose high into the sky.

Uncle Bill reclaimed the glasses and nodded toward the woods. "It's dry as the Sahara out there," he said. "If those poor trees could talk, they'd be crying for rain. A thunderstorm, a shower, anything wet would help. Now let's climb down the ladder and take a walk in the woods. Show you what I mean."

CHAPTER 3
DRY AS A CAMEL'S COAT

While the Mitchell brothers and their uncle were tramping through the still woods, back in Haileybury—at the corner of Main Street and Ferguson Avenue—several women sat around a table on the open balcony of the Maple Leaf Hotel. They were sipping iced tea from tall glasses and fanning themselves with luncheon menus.

The torrid weather had been the main topic of conversation among the shoppers who walked along Main Street and those who rode the trolley cars that ran for ten miles from Cobalt in the south to New Liskeard in the north. Haileybury was situated in the middle, hugging the shore of Lake Temiskaming. The weekend fishermen, who perched on the long dock that stretched far out into the lake, lazily cast their lines into the water and complained about the heat wave. "It's killed all my worms and all the fish are on the bottom, asleep in the deep, their fins pulled over their eyes," one of them sighed. Others on the dock awaited the arrival of the paddlewheeler Alexandria, the largest of the boats to ply the waters of the 60-mile lake.

"Let's enjoy this weather while we can," said Amy Mitchell to her friends. "I remember last year at this time I was out buying long underwear for Max and Marty. Remember how cold and wet and miserable it was? It won't be long before we'll be buried under snow."

"There's never been a fall like this one," Bernice Arnold, the undertaker's wife, said, dabbing discreetly at a drop of perspiration on her upper lip. "The hot weather is almost unbearable."

Amy was the youngest in the group and the most vivacious. Unlike the others, she held down a job, helping her husband Harry at the *Haileyburian*. Amy also found time in her busy schedule to curl in winter, golf in summer, play bridge like a world champion, tend her garden, and raise two boys—Max and Marty. Amy was by far the town's best female skater and hockey player. At one time, she had been described in newspaper accounts as "one of the premier lady hockeyists in North America." That was after she had led her team—the Snowflakes— through three consecutive undefeated seasons. The Snowflakes' record during that span was 36-0 and Amy was credited with 82 of her team's 146 goals.

After the Snowflakes captured the North American Women's Championship and the Lady Stanley Cup, Amy was named MVP of the tournament. During the tournament, she met Harry Mitchell, a dashing young reporter who covered the hockey beat for his newspaper—the *North Country Nugget*. He wrote a feature story about her, they began dating and a year later they were married. The following year, Harry borrowed some money and bought the *Haileyburian*.

Max had inherited his mother's hockey skills. He was the best teenage player in town. Everyone said so, even Amy. "He's very good," she would state candidly when asked, "and he'll get a lot better. But if his hockey success ever goes to his head, if he begins to think he's another Charlie Conacher or Howie Morenz, then he'll have to answer to me. And that goes for Marty, too. He's beginning to show a lot of promise." With Amy for a mother there wasn't much chance that Max or Marty's heads would swell for any reason but natural growth.

"Where are your boys today, Amy?" Bernice inquired. "Out breaking the hearts of all the teenage girls in town?"

Amy laughed. "No, Max and Marty cycled out to the fire tower. They're working on a story for the *Haileyburian*."

"So they are interested in something other than sports?" Bernice asked, smiling. "It seems every time

17

I see them they've got skates and a stick over their shoulders."

"Or a baseball bat and a glove," countered Amy.

Meanwhile, in the deep forest far from town, in the shadow of the fire tower, forest ranger Bill Mitchell and his nephews Max and Marty tramped through the woods. The ranger pointed out the various species of trees and plants, and when he stepped on a rotted log, it split apart.

"Hey, there must be a million ants living in there," Marty said, crouching down to see the tiny insects scurrying in all directions. "Now they've got no home."

"Don't worry about them," chuckled Uncle Bill. "They'll be back, as tenacious as ever. Ants are remarkable survivors. They've been around for over 100 million years. Scientists estimate there are a quadrillion ants alive on earth.

"A quadrillion?" said Marty, his eyes wide. "How many is that?"

Uncle Bill chuckled. "Let me put it this way. Next time you have a picnic and ants come around, tell them to leave all their relatives at home. Or you'll be buried under a mountain of them."

Just then, in the distance, they heard a strange noise, like a cry for help.

"What was that?" asked Max.

"Sounded like the bawling of a cow moose," Uncle Bill said. "This is mating season for moose and the cow is probably trying to attract a mate."

"Can we go see it?" Marty asked.

"No, it's pretty far away. And moose like to be left alone. They're marvelous animals. They can swim ten or 12 miles without stopping and they eat about 50 pounds of twigs every day. Did you know the males grow huge antlers that fall off in winter?"

"The antlers fall off?"

"Yep. But they grow back again in the spring." The ranger and his nephews walked through some dry leaves that crackled underfoot.

"The forest is a tinderbox," said Uncle Bill. "The forest floor is usually spongy and moist. Now it's as hard and dry as a camel's coat. Here it is late September when we often get freezing rain and snow. Almost time to get our hockey gear out, right? Yet it's still like midsummer out here. Stifling."

"What causes most forest fires, Uncle Bill?" Max asked, his pencil poised.

"Often it's careless hunters or fishermen. Someone who doesn't have the common sense to put a campfire out. I mean completely out."

"What else?" Max asked.

"Well, there's lightning. A bolt of lightning can crack open a thick pine. The tree starts blazing. Other trees can't run away so they burn too. First thing you know, the whole forest is on fire."

"Where do the animals go when the forest burns?" Marty asked.

"They make a run for it. Try to survive. Birds are lucky because they can fly away. Snakes and small animals will slither into their holes. Beaver families will huddle inside their homes in the middle of a pond. If the flames come close they'll glide under water, sharing pond space with turtles and fish. Many animals suffocate when the fire steals the oxygen they need to breathe."

"What happens when people get caught in forest fires?" Marty asked.

"It can be heart breaking. Lots of farmers have been burned out," Uncle Bill said solemnly. "A friend of mine had 100 acres up near Chilcott a couple of years ago. Lost it all to a fire—the house, the barn, the farm animals, everything. He and his family had to go underground for a couple of days."

"Underground?" said Marty.

"That's right. Into what's called a root house. It's really just a hole dug in the side of a hill. The family huddled in there, in pitch darkness, as wisps of smoke crept under the barricaded door. The children clung to each other and prayed to God, asking Him to spare their lives."

"Oh, my gosh," murmured Marty.

Marty had a vivid imagination. In his mind, he

pictured the children coughing and sucking in the foul air. Marty pictured himself among them, wishing he were anywhere but in a stuffy old root house. Afraid he was going to suffocate and die, wishing he were safe in his bed, dreaming sweet dreams of riding ponies or fishing for trout.

He took a deep breath of fresh air and realized that Uncle Bill was still talking.

"Hours later, when the fury of the flames moved away, the survivors crept outside, blinking through tears, gasping for breath and thirsty for water. They were shocked when they looked around them. Everything familiar was gone; the fine house their father had built of logs, the outbuildings, and the crops, even the freshly painted doghouse. Burned to the ground. Even so, they were thankful for one thing—they were still alive."

"Wow!" Marty exclaimed. His uncle was a great storyteller. "I've never seen a root house," he said. "Not in Haileybury."

"That's easy to explain. Most towns today are protected from forest fires by farmland or wasteland on the outskirts of town—land stripped of trees. People in town don't need root houses. You know the Dooley brothers? Mayor Pringle's wife Mabel insisted they be hired—they're her brothers after all. They've been working hard cutting dead wood and brush around Haileybury. When they get finished, there'll be a nice firebreak between the forest and the town. He stopped talking.

"Why are you two grinning?"

"We know the Dooleys," Max explained, "They've never worked hard in their lives."

"Unless it's over a pool table," Marty added. "Uncle Bill, what happened to your friend? Did he give up farming? Did he move to a safer place?"

"Yes, he moved," said Uncle Bill. "But he didn't give up. People in the North Country don't give up. Most of us are determined to carry on no matter what Mother Nature throws at us."

Back in the tower, Marty raised the camera and said, "Look at me and say please." Uncle Bill began to laugh. "Don't you mean cheese, Marty?" He looked at Max and winked. Then he said, "Marty, try turning the camera around. The lens has to be pointing at me, not you." Marty looked down and grinned. "Oops, my mistake." He snapped off several photos of his uncle.

"Now one more," he pleaded, "this time with you looking for fires through your binoculars."

Uncle Bill chuckled, lifted the glasses and scanned the horizon. Behind him the camera clicked. Then he said, "Uh oh." In the distance he saw flashes of lightning dance over the tree line. "We don't need lightning," he murmured. "We need rain."

He turned the glasses in another direction and stopped. "That's funny," he said.

"What is it, Uncle Bill?" the boys asked, almost in unison.

"Over there," he said, pointing. "A few miles northwest of Haileybury. Thought I saw a wee wisp of smoke rise in the air. It's probably nothing. Never mind, lads. You be on your way. It's a long way back home."

The boys said their goodbyes and scrambled down the ladder. When Marty was about halfway from the bottom he slipped on a rung and fell the rest of the way, landing on his backside.

"I told you to be careful on that ladder," Uncle Bill yelled from above. "Are you all right, Marty?"

Marty jumped up and hopped around in circles, rubbing his behind and muttering to himself. Then he looked up and yelled, "I'm okay, Uncle Bill. Got a bit of a sore bum, is all."

Neither Max nor his uncle could contain themselves. They broke into laughter. Soon Marty was laughing too.

CHAPTER 4

A STRANGER COMES ASHORE

When the Mitchell boys arrived back in town, they saw Isaac Watters' ice wagon pulled up in front of their house on Marcella Street.

"Let's get some slivers of ice," Marty suggested. They dropped their bikes on their front lawn and ran to the back of the wagon. Isaac—everybody called him "Iceman"—greeted them. "Hot enough for you fellows?" he asked. Using metal tongs, Iceman was busy shifting several large blocks of ice, cut from the lake in winter and packed in sawdust in a large icehouse, to the back of the wagon. He had plenty of customers in the neighbourhood.

"Guess I know what you two are after on a hot day like this. Well, help yourself."

The boys found several chunks of loose ice in the wagon. Each boy grabbed a sliver and began sucking on it. It was cool and refreshing. Water rolled down their chins and covered their hands.

The Iceman grinned. He was used to kids hounding him for scraps of ice. "Your mom's not home," Iceman told the boys. "Kitchen door was open so I put a 50-pound block in her icebox. Tell her she owes me 25 cents. I'll collect next week, okay?" He climbed in the front of his wagon, clucked his tongue, said gently, "Go, Homer." The horse obediently moved on to the next customer.

When the boys entered the house through the back door they saw a note on the kitchen table.

Max and Marty:

I'm meeting the ladies for tea at the Maple Leaf Hotel. When you get back from your visit with Uncle Bill, come down to the hotel. I'll meet you in the lobby at four. We'll go to Liggett's for ice cream. Love, Mom.

The boys went to the bathroom to wash up. They slicked their hair back, changed their shirts, ran for their bikes and headed downtown. There was no need to rush but they hurried anyway. It was always fun to sit on the steps of the Maple Leaf and watch the world go by. That's what they planned to do while they were waiting for their mother.

When the boys arrived at the Maple Leaf, they leaned their bicycles against a board fence and went to sit on the steps of the hotel. From the lobby they could hear the sounds of a piano. Someone was playing the latest Broadway hits and playing them well.

In the middle of the empty street, several men

stood in a group, arguing noisily. They were debating the salary earned by baseball slugger Babe Ruth, who had just retired after 20 seasons as the home run king with 714. "It was insane for the Yankees to pay Ruth 60,000 dollars a season," one old prospector griped. "That's more than the President of the United States got paid."

"But Babe hit 60 homers in 1927," another prospector argued. "And he had millions more fans than the President. Like Ruth said himself—I had a better year than the President."

"Aw, he was just another ball player—an overpaid prima donna," muttered the older prospector.

"Like heck he was," the second prospector snorted angrily. "Why, they'd never have had Yankee Stadium if it wasn't for Ruth. They even call it the House that Ruth Built. He never turned down a kid's request for an autograph. And another thing I'll bet you don't know about the Babe. He was the first ball player to order a bat with a knob on the end. Now every bat is made with one."

"I should never have thrown my old ball glove and bat away," a heavyset man in his mid-twenties moaned. "If I'd stuck at it I could have been a slugger like Ruth."

Max nudged Marty. "Look! It's Elmer Dooley. Bragging about what a great ball player he was. He and his brother Barney have their hunting jackets on. Looks like they've just come in from the bush."

"Is Babe Ruth a fat guy...like Elmer?" Marty asked.

"Yeah. Kinda fat. But 100 times a better ball player than Elmer. Elmer's slow. He quit playing ball when a little kid grabbed his base hit in centre field and threw him out."

"Where? At home plate?"

"No. At first base."

Elmer and Barney Dooley were known as braggarts, bullies and all-round troublemakers.

"Elmer, you only look like Babe Ruth," someone told him. "Fat and bowlegged."

The comment prompted a roar of laughter.

"What trouble are you Dooleys going to find yourselves in today?" Noah Miller asked. Noah worked the night shift at the Busy Bee restaurant—a short order cook. He loved needling the Dooleys. "By the way, where have you two been the last couple of days? Haven't seen you in the Busy Bee. We rely on your big appetites to keep us in business."

"We been doin' a little hunting, doin' a little prospecting," Elmer said with a shrug.

"Hunting?" Noah Miller roared, slapping his thigh. "If you two went moose hunting it's a wonder you didn't shoot each other. The size of you two. If you had antlers where your ears are, you wouldn't last a day in the woods." Again, everybody laughed at Noah's witty remark—everybody but the Dooleys.

"Now as for prospecting," Noah continued, playing to his audience. "Boys, can you picture these two Einsteins—fellows who wouldn't know silver ore from a strawberry sundae—going out prospecting? That's a good one." There was more laughter at Noah Miller's jibe.

"Did you remember to bring stakes with you?" someone asked.

"We brought hot dogs and buns," Barney Dooley said.

There was another great roar of laughter.

"He meant survey stakes—not beef steaks," Noah howled gleefully.

The Dooleys looked at each other. Elmer said, "We didn't bring any kind of stakes."

"But what if you two famous prospectors had stumbled on a silver mine out there in the bush? You'd have had to walk back to your car, then drive into town to get some stakes."

"That's all right. We'd have done it," Elmer said.

"We're good walkers," Barney added. "But hey, we were lucky. We never stumbled on a silver mine. So there."

The men slapped their knees and laughed some more, even though Barney thought he'd given them all a pretty good answer.

"I hear you two were seen panning for gold in Mabel Pringle's lily pond," Noah added, winking at his buddies. "Did you find some ore there?"

"No, we never done that," Elmer said, scratching his ear and shuffling back and forth on his big feet. "We're not that dumb."

"Well, did you two find anything at all while you were away hunting and prospecting—and shirking your duties?" Noah asked.

"Shirking? What's shirking?" Barney asked.

Elmer poked Barney in the ribs to silence him.

"Yeah, we found something," he said to the grinning faces. "We found that when all the ice melts in the cooler, the beer gets warm and you have to drink it faster. And when all the bottles are empty that means it's time to come home."

Elmer was proud of himself for making a joke. And prouder still when everyone roared at his clever remark.

"Hey Elmer!" Noah Miller shouted. "Let's get serious. Did you and your brother ever finish clearing the land outside of town for a firebreak? You know, fit it into your busy schedule? You remember it, don't you? The cushy job you started weeks ago, the one you're trying to stretch into the next century?"

Elmer grinned.

"Almost done, Noah. Almost done. Give us a few more days. My brother Barney and I, your humble public servants, will be back at work tomorrow. We promise to keep all of you safe from any bushfires.

Say, did you hear what happened the other day? Barney and I stumbled onto a cave in the woods, right next to the Johnston farm. We figure some bears have been living in it. There were prints all around. It was kind of scary being in there, looking around."

Noah laughed. "If a bear ate you boys up, he'd have enough in his belly to last him a lifetime. Plus a bad case of indigestion. But I guess if a bear ate the Dooleys, Mayor Pringle would pop open the champagne and celebrate."

"Why would he do that?" asked Elmer. "Because he wouldn't have to pay for any more jobs his wife decides you two workaholics should have. You're her brothers, aren't you?"

"Yeah. Both of us."

There was more laughter but Noah's last barb had struck a nerve. Elmer and Barney were stuck for an answer so they simply stood there, shuffling their feet and feeling foolish.

The conversation trailed off when one of the town's new trolley cars rolled by. The men were curious to see who got on and who got off. Trolleys were relatively new to Haileybury and still drew a lot of attention. The Mitchell boys and their friends sometimes rode the trolley back and forth even though they had no destination in mind. The fare for kids was only a nickel.

Suddenly, the men stopped talking. They heard the "Whoo-oot" of a ship's horn echo across the lake. They turned to watch the huge paddle wheeler Alexandria; its decks loaded with passengers and supplies, nose its way toward the long wharf.

"Lets see how Old Wharfbuster makes out today," cackled Noah, a navy veteran from the Great War. "He's about an hour late today and he's comin' in awful fast."

"So what else is new?" said Elmer Dooley. "Those people on the dock had better step back."

The Mitchell brothers leaped up when they heard the blare of the paddle wheeler's horn. From their vantage point, they had a perfect view of the stubby ship approaching the shoreline. Moments later, the ship banged heavily into its mooring place beside the dock. The men on shore roared with laughter when they saw the dock shake and tremble from the blow. They laughed harder when a couple of dock timbers were reduced to splinters. The Alexandria finally shuddered to a stop. White paint had been stripped from her bow as a result of the collision, a hard, ugly landing that had forced people standing nearby to jump back in alarm.

The ship was quickly moored with ropes as thick as baseball bats before any further damage could be sustained. Curses common to seafaring men could be heard and they appeared to come from the ship's bridge.

The Alexandria was well known throughout the North Country. Her captain, Amos Warbister, commander of a merchant ship during World War I, had become a legend up and down Lake Temiskaming. Most folks called him Old Wharfbuster behind his back because of his spectacular landings. Occasionally, the vibrations from the blow when a determined prow met an unyielding wharf sent unwary passengers somersaulting along the ship's deck. Sometimes they'd even be pitched over the ship's bow, to land in the water or in the arms of strangers below, people who themselves were fighting for balance on the swaying wharf. The onlookers on shore always laughed uproariously. It was great fun to watch Old Wharfbuster at work.

"The old captain has bad eyes," Noah Miller said.

"Yeah, and a bad habit of drinking on the job," said Elmer. "That stuff he guzzles doesn't improve his vision or his judgment."

"Nor does it yours and Barney's," Noah quipped, referring to the Dooleys' love of liquid refreshment.

The captain appeared on the upper deck. He wore thick glasses and a white uniform with gold braid on his shoulders. More gold braid lined his cap. Grinning broadly, he waved to the people on the dock and on the shore. Warbister loved an audience. Everyone gave him a cheer. He'd just guided the

Alexandria up and down the lake for the umpteenth time. Not a great landing, he'd have to agree, but he'd seen worse. Everything was hunky-dory except for some lost paint and another small dent in the bow of his vessel.

"Way to go, Captain Wharfbuster!" Marty shouted, clapping his hands. "Way to go, sir."

"Hush, Marty," Max hissed, nudging his brother with an elbow. "I think he heard you."

Indeed, the good captain had heard Marty's comment but had failed to note either the sarcasm or the fact his name had been mispronounced.

He snapped off a salute toward the hotel and bellowed, "I can't see you, lad, but I thank you. It's nice to be appreciated."

The men standing in the street laughed uproariously.

All of the passengers who disembarked from the Alexandria had to withstand the scrutiny of the local residents. It had become a ritual. It was only natural to be curious about newcomers to town. Many of the visitors had relatives waiting and were whisked away by car or horse and buggy to homes in the community. Others burdened with packsacks and suitcases made their way up the hill to the hotels on Main Street. One passenger hoisted a canoe over his head and started up the hill. Another drew hoots from the crowd when he tossed a pair of snowshoes over his back.

"Did you think this place was the North Pole?" Elmer asked mockingly, as the man drew near.

"You should have brought your bathing suit," said Noah Miller. "And your suntan lotion."

Embarrassed and cowed, the man smiled but said nothing. He walked on, happy to be putting distance between himself and the local hecklers.

One passenger, a tall man wearing a pink shirt under a wrinkled suit, stopped abruptly when the Dooley brothers stepped in front of him and blocked his path. He gave them a menacing look, a glare that stopped all laughter and prompted them to step back. "Thank you, gentlemen," he said cordially, tipping his hat.

On the steps of the hotel, Max nudged his brother. "The Dooleys had better not fool around with that fellow," he whispered. "Did you see the look in his eyes?"

The stranger turned and sniffed the air. "I smell smoke," he said, staring straight into the grinning face of Elmer Dooley. "There must be a few forest fires burning around here. Anything a fellow has to worry about?"

"Aw, there's a few small fires burning west of here," Noah Miller replied before Elmer could respond. "But nothin' to worry about, mister. If you go out in the bush and come across one, don't get scairt. You just whistle, mister. We'll come runnin'.'"

"Sometimes we have to pee on it," Elmer said imp-
ishly and everyone chuckled.

Encouraged, he added, "I'm the champion around
here. Want a demonstration?"

"Some other time," replied the solemn stranger, as
he moved through the group and turned toward the
hotel. Just then he appeared to stumble and one of
his heavy boots came down hard on Elmer's toe.
"Holy mackinaw, that hurt!" howled Elmer, who
hopped around on one foot while his pals laughed.
The stranger didn't laugh. He took Elmer by the
elbow and squeezed hard, saying, "Mister, I'm real
sorry about your toe. But surely you know it was an
accident, right?"

He squeezed a little harder. Elmer nodded his
head and winced in pain. Now his body hurt in two
places. He pulled away and said, "Right, mister. It
was an accident. You bet. I'm real sorry I got in
your way."

The man turned toward the hotel. Then he
stopped and said over his shoulder, "Say, fella, did
anyone ever tell you that you look like Babe Ruth,
the ball player?"

He didn't wait for a reply. He wouldn't have heard
it anyway over the laughter from the crowd of men.

On the steps of the hotel the man sat down next to

the Mitchell boys, took off his black hat and fanned his face. Without turning his head, the stranger said quietly, "You boys got any smart aleck comments to add to what I just heard?"

"No sir," the boys replied in unison.

"Seems to me you taught Elmer Dooley a good lesson," Marty murmured. "Some of us kids call Elmer and his brother the Dopey Dooleys."

The stranger looked surprised. "You say that to their faces?"

Marty laughed. "No, sir. Never to their faces. They'd kill us if we did."

The man put a hand to his ear. "Where's that music coming from?" he asked.

Max grinned. "That's Mrs. Stratten at the piano. She's inside—in the lobby. Her husband died in a mine accident last year. She comes here almost every day to play the songs he liked. She can play anything."

"Yep, she's dern good," said the stranger. "I haven't heard much music lately—not where I've been."

"And where was that?" asked Marty.

"Oh, nowhere special." Then he changed the subject. "You want to earn a dime?" the stranger asked.

"Sure. What do we have to do?"

"Go back to the Alexandria and pick up a package I left on board. Tell the steward it's for Mr. Jamison. Jesse Jamison."

The boys leaped off the steps and ran to the wharf. They were back in minutes with the package.

"Thanks, fellas," the stranger said, taking the package and flipping a quarter in their direction. Max caught it expertly.

"Good catch," said Mr. Jamison. "Keep the change. Say, you boys got names?"

"Yes sir," Max replied. "We're the Mitchell brothers. I'm Max and this is Marty."

The man pulled a gold watch from his pocket and glanced at it. He looked disgusted. "That fool friend of mine is never on time," he said with a sigh.

"Your friend's supposed to meet you?" Marty asked.

"Yep. Said he'd drive down from Englehart to pick me up. Probably got into some kind of trouble on the way. This guy is always in trouble. Not an easy man to get along with." He grinned and looked at the boys. "I haven't seen my pal in a long time." He looked around. "I know this town and all the towns around here. I grew up in the North Country. Used to know every inch of this country." He tossed the package high in the air, and then caught it expertly. "If he doesn't come soon I'll just keep these cigars for myself." He cupped his eyes and peered down Main Street. "Englehart isn't far away. It's not like he's coming from Alaska. What's keeping that so-and-so?"

Just then a yellow car came racing down the street, dust flying in all directions. The driver blasted the horn, forcing the men still loitering in the street to leap out of the way. Marty smiled. He'd never seen them move so fast—especially the Dooleys.

"Look at them scatter!" Mr. Jamison laughed, slapping his thigh.

He stood up and waved as the driver of the car roared past the hotel, made a U turn that sent more dust flying as high as the rooftops. The driver hit the brake and the car screeched to a stop. "That's my crazy partner," Mr. Jamison said, grabbing his suitcase and running to the car. "See you later, fellas. Stay away from the bad guys."

When he reached the yellow car and yanked the door open, the boys could hear Mr. Jamison chastising the driver for his tardiness. "You moron, Bert. What kept you?" He growled, throwing his suitcase into the back seat.

"Hey, Jesse, wasn't my fault," the man replied angrily. "Had a flat tire just outside of town. And before that I had a real problem with a couple of stupid kids along the way. They forced me off the road and almost killed me…"

Max leaped to his feet. "Marty, that's the crazy guy we met on the way to the tower. Look, it's the same car—a yellow Buick."

A door slammed and the automobile sped off down the street.

"And it's the same licence number," Marty exclaimed. "Begins with PU. Darn it, I still can't make out the rest of it. Anyway, I hope he goes back to Englehart and stays there."

"What's all the commotion, boys? And who's the reckless driver—the one who almost knocked the Dooley boys into the lake?"

The boys turned. Their mother had just come from the lobby of the hotel.

"Oh, hi, Mom. We helped a stranger," Marty explained. "He gave us a whole quarter—just to run an errand."

"Too bad the Dooleys weren't knocked into the lake," Max said. "They'd have had their first bath in weeks."

Amy Mitchell gave her sons a hug and said, "Good deeds should be rewarded. Sounds like he was a generous man."

"He was," Max agreed. "But there was something about him that bothers me."

"Like what, son?"

"Oh, I don't know. A feeling he was up to something he didn't want to tell us about. And he didn't want to tell us where he came from or where he was going. I think he might have been in jail or something."

"Really?" their mother said.

"Yeah, Mom," said Marty. "And we sure didn't like the guy who came to pick him up, the driver who almost made mincemeat of the Dooleys. He's a real menace behind the wheel of a car."

"Well, then," said their mother. "It's a good thing they're on their way and out of your lives forever. You'll probably never see either one of them again. Now then, how about a trip to the ice cream counter? On our way we can stop in at the newspaper. Perhaps your father can join us."

CHAPTER 5

A NATURAL ATHLETE

For the most part, Marty and Max got along like best friends. Kids at school sometimes teased Max about why he spent so much time with his kid brother Marty. After all, most teenagers in town avoided their younger siblings like poison ivy. Max said he didn't mind having Marty tag along. He was a good kid and he was always doing something to make Max laugh. Besides, there weren't many kids in the neighbourhood who were Marty's age.

Lately, though, things had changed. Max was spending less time with Marty and more time with Sally Logan.

"What's the big deal with Sally?" he asked Max one day.

"No big deal. Sally's smart and fun to be with and great to talk to," Max answered.

"Like I'm not?"

"Marty, you're a great brother. But sometimes I

like to talk about other things than hockey and base-ball and building a tree house. Sally and I talk about all kinds of things."

"Oh, like dancing and movie stars and the latest pop tunes on the radio?"

"Sure, why not? Sometimes we talk about careers and what we hope to achieve in life. And we talk about our families. Now that's enough prying. What Sally and I talk about is really nobody's business but ours. You're not jealous, are you?"

"Course not," Marty said, looking away. "But Agnes Witherspoon sure is."

"You're kidding. Agnes is Sally's best friend."

"Sure she is. Or pretends to be. But I've seen the looks she gives you two when you're together."

"Looks?"

"Glares, then. Agnes thinks you should be chasing her around the schoolyard, not Sally. She'd love to be in Sally's place."

"Marty, don't be ridiculous," Max said, laughing. "I don't chase Sally around the schoolyard. And I don't give two hoots for Agnes Witherspoon."

"I know you don't. That's the trouble. And if any-one knows about troublemaking, it's Agnes. Remember I said so. Just be careful, Romeo."

Smoke hung over the community all week and sev-eral parents of young children kept them home from school. Max had football practice every afternoon, and on Friday, before a crowd of 400 students and parents, he quarterbacked Haileybury High to a thrilling 21-7 victory over arch rival New Liskeard, passing for two touchdowns and scoring another himself on an 85-yard run. Marty ran along the sidelines, snapping photos whenever Max carried the ball. He even took a shot of Sally in her cheerleading costume, and laughed when he caught her while she was wiping her nose in a hankie.

His coach at Haileybury High said Max was a natural athlete, one of the best he'd ever seen. He was the star pitcher on the Haileybury Ravens baseball team and held three school records in track and field. But his favourite sport was hockey. Last season, as team captain of the Hawks, the town's junior club, he'd scored 30 goals, added 42 assists and captured the league's MVP award.

A pro scout, Mr. Davidson, had journeyed all the way from Toronto to see him perform on the ice. After the game in which Max scored all three goals for the Hawks, the scout had come back to the Mitchell house and rung the doorbell. Marty put down the Hardy Boys book he'd been reading and invited him in. The man beamed when Marty asked him for his autograph; even though Marty had no idea he'd been a star in the NHL. The scout had a deep scar over his lip, a souvenir of some long ago hockey injury when he'd played for the famous

Toronto Arenas, winners of the Stanley Cup in 1918.

Everyone sat around the kitchen table. Mrs. Mitchell poured hot tea and passed out her home-made peanut butter cookies. Mr. Davidson wanted to get right down to business. He was returning to Toronto by rail and his train left in an hour.

"Max, my boy, you put on some muscle and we'll bring you to Toronto and put you into junior hockey there," the scout promised. He smiled and waited for Max to reply. Most teens were speechless when told a pro team might be interested in them.

"Mr. Davidson, do you really think I'm good enough to play with the best young players in Toronto?" he asked.

"Sure I do."

"And where would I live in Toronto?"

"We'd find a place for you. A billet."

"A billet? What's a billet?" Marty interjected.

"A billet is a home where people look after young players. It's like they adopt them temporarily."

"Oh."

Mrs. Mitchell signalled Marty to hush. Let the man talk to Max.

"Oh, there's another thing." Davidson pulled a billfold from his jacket pocket. He licked his finger and began placing a number of small bills on the table, directly in front of Max. There were several fives, some twos, a couple of tens and finally, a new

20-dollar bill. He beamed at the Mitchells. Then he leaned toward Max. "There's 100 dollars for you, lad," he said. "One hundred smackers." He fumbled for some paper in another pocket. "This is your lucky day, son. All you have to do to earn all this money is sign this form, which binds you to our team."

"For how long?" Max asked. His eyes were on the scout, not on the money or the paper. The scout frowned. Most kids didn't ask about the length of a contract. But they all asked how much? They couldn't wait to snatch up the money.

"Why, for as long as you play hockey," the man replied.

Mr. Mitchell puffed on his pipe, listening intently. He was curious to know how Max would respond.

"Gee," Max said, frowning. "I don't know what to say, Mr. Davidson. I'm not sure I'd want a team to own me. For my entire career? What if I wanted to play for some other team—let's say in Detroit or New York? I couldn't do that, could I?"

"I'm afraid not, Max. Not unless we traded you there."

Max frowned. He thought for a moment, and then said to the scout, "Mr. Davidson, I'm really flattered. But Toronto? It's such a big city and I really love it here in Haileybury." When he thought of leaving the Hawks, his brother, his parents, his pals at school and a girl named Sally, his stomach churned. He needed some time to think about the offer, time to talk it over with his folks. And with Sally. He was surprised that the idea of moving all the way to Toronto and playing hockey there didn't excite him much more than it did. Three or four young men from the area had made it all the way to the National Hockey League and when they returned in the summer months to play ball and work at the brewery, they were big men in town. Celebrities.

Marty tried to kick Max under the table. Marty rolled his eyes and coughed and when Max glanced over at him, his brother mouthed the words "Sign the paper. Take the money." Max couldn't read lips but he got the message. It made him smile. Finally Max said, "It's a really tempting offer, sir. But look, I'm still pretty young. I love hockey but I'm not sure about the game as a career. I thought I might become a geologist someday. Or maybe a forest ranger or even a bush pilot. I'm going to have to think about this for a few days. And of course I want to know what my folks think about it, too. I enjoy helping them out by working on the paper."

Mr. Mitchell finally spoke. "Max, you're wise not to rush into anything. If you're good enough for top level junior hockey now you'll be even better a year from now." He turned to the scout and smiled.

"Thank you for coming, sir. We're pleased you think so highly of Max. We've always known he was special. In fact, we think both of our boys are special." Marty beamed and pushed out his chest. He raised both arms like a boxer celebrating a win. He stopped when his mother said, "Marty, enough..."

"So we'll discuss the matter and come to a decision in a few days," Mr. Mitchell said.

"Does that mean he's not going to leave all this money?" asked Marty, hooking a thumb toward the scout.

Everyone chuckled. "You've got it, Marty," Mr. Mitchell said.

Marty was bitterly disappointed in Max. Later, when they were bringing in wood from the shed for the kitchen stove, Marty spit on the woodpile and muttered, "I didn't know I had such a dumb brother. Do you know how many things you can buy for 100 dollars? I think you just lost all your marbles tonight that's what I think. It's a wonder they weren't rolling around on the kitchen floor."

Max laughed. "A hundred bucks won't get you much—not these days. You know I love hockey, Marty, but it's still just a game. Mom and Dad need our help. Look at it this way. If the *New York Times* called you tomorrow and offered you a job as a photographer, you wouldn't be on the next midnight train out of Haileybury, would you?"

"Sure I would. That's where we're different. I'd be gone with the wind. Off to make fame and fortune."

"I don't believe you. And if you did get such an offer, you'd be back home in a week, homesick and hungry. Scared to death of big city life."

"That's bull. And the next time Mr. Davidson comes to the North Country, it's going to be me he signs. And I'll ask him for a 1,000 dollars."

A few days later, when Mr. Davidson called long distance from Toronto, Max told him politely that yes, he'd made up his mind. He'd decided to remain in Haileybury for at least another year. "I really should help my Mom and Dad with the newspaper," he explained. "If I take money from a pro team it may cost me a chance to get a scholarship to a university. I think I should wait at least another year." Mr. Davidson sighed and said he was disappointed but he understood and wished Max well. He added, "But I'll be back, young man. I'd hate to lose a young man with your potential. And by the way, why not bring your folks and that brother of yours to a pro game this winter? The club will pay all expenses. Be our guests at the new Maple Leaf Gardens." Max said he was thrilled to be invited and immediately told his family the good news.

CHAPTER 6

A BANK HEIST IN ENGLEHART

Several miles to the north of Haileybury, in the small town of Englehart, two men in a yellow, dust-covered Buick drove slowly down the tranquil main street. Even though it was hot and the air inside the car was stifling, the men wore hats pulled low over their heads. The car came to a stop in front of the town's only bank. The men looked carefully up and down the street before stepping out of the car. They tossed their cigar butts into the dirt and stepped on them.

The sweltering midday sun was keeping most people indoors or in their gardens. It was so quiet the men could almost hear the snip of the clippers through the open window of the barbershop across the street.

The bulky, red-faced man who'd been driving the car turned to his slimmer companion. "What do you think, Jesse?"

"I think it's time. Should be a piece of cake. Nobody's around, Bert. A lot of the men have gone north to fight a small forest fire. Let's just do it."

"If we're caught, it's back to the slammer for both of us. We'll have to serve ten years for sure next time. That's a lot of time behind bars."

"Stop talkin' Bert. We're not going to get caught. Don't lose your nerve on me now. I say let's go."

"We bringing the rifle? It's under the blanket in the back seat."

"We won't need it. I told you that already. Pistol's all we need."

The men entered the bank and approached the lone teller on duty, a young man wearing thick glasses. He was a mousy fellow afflicted with poor eyesight and protruding ears. He was involved in a losing struggle with acne.

"Hi, son. Is the manager in?" Jesse asked.

"Sure is," the youth replied. Jesse noticed the teller's teeth needed attention too. The youth called over his shoulder to someone in a small office, "Hey, Dad. Man wants to see you."

A grownup version of the teller stepped briskly from the office. He smiled his banker's smile, even though he was inwardly annoyed. His lunch had just been interrupted. He moved to the counter and said, "Gentlemen, the name is Baldwin. Clarence S.

Baldwin. The handsome young man at the counter is Cyril S. Baldwin. Now, how may I be of service?" Baldwin the elder had his son's ears, Jesse noted, but straighter teeth and smooth pink skin. His best feature, Jesse thought.

"Just the two of you on duty today?" Jesse asked politely.

"We have another employee who is currently at lunch. Her name, I'm pleased to say, is Priscilla S. Baldwin. Prissy is due back in twenty minutes."

Jesse said, "Sir, my friend and I have come for some money."

"Quite a lot of money," added Bert, grinning through his tobacco stained teeth.

"Indeed. You want to borrow money. For a new car, a mining venture, some property perhaps?"

"Did I say borrow?" Jesse said, turning to wink at Bert.

Bert said, "I didn't hear no borrow. No sir, Mr. Baldwin, we want all your money," Bert stepped forward and grabbed the astonished banker by the throat with one meaty hand. He dragged Clarence S. Baldwin across the counter until their noses almost touched.

Jesse, meanwhile, had pulled a large revolver from his pocket and pointed it at the teller, Cyril S. Baldwin, whose mouth was agape. His eyes rolled around behind his glasses.

"Geez..." said Bert fascinated. "Will ya look at those eyes..."

"Lie down on the floor, Cyril, and be quick about it," Jesse barked. He waved his gun and the teller dropped like a stone. His head smacked into the hardwood floor and his glasses flew off. Jesse smiled and deliberately stepped on the spectacles. "Oops," he said softly. Jesse looked down at the youth and noticed poor Cyril was about to start crying. And it looked like he'd wet his pants a little.

"You cover the door," he ordered Bert. "Give me the banker." He grabbed the banker by the wrist, twisting it cruelly, and forced him to walk back to the vault. "Open the safe, Baldwin!" he snarled. "And don't tell me you don't know the combination. We've been in here before. We've seen you do it." It was a lie, but Clarence Baldwin wasn't about to debate the claim.

The banker obediently worked on the combination with trembling fingers. In seconds the safe flew open. Jesse pulled a soft leather bag from under his shirt. "Fill it up!" he demanded and the banker complied. Hundreds of bills of all denominations were stuffed into the bag.

By the front door, Bert was growing nervous. This was taking too long. "Let's go, Jesse. There's a lady coming from across the street."

Jesse pushed the banker's face to the floor and

placed the gun barrel against his pink cheek. "You and your boy stay flat as a board for ten minutes, hear me? Not a peep out of you. Don't even breathe. You got that, Baldwin?"

"Yes sir," the banker mumbled. "We won't breathe." He closed his eyes, puffed out his cheeks and lay still as a corpse. His pink skin was quickly turning to the colour of paste.

Jesse vaulted over the counter and ran to the door. Through the glass he saw a lady approaching. She was fishing for something in her purse, her bankbook perhaps. Bert and Jesse stepped outside into the bright sunlight. Jesse had worked the lock on the door so that when he closed it behind him it could not be re-opened — not from the outside.

"Lean on me, Bert," Jesse whispered. "And look sick."

He put his arm around Bert's waist and Bert, taking his cue, rested his head on Jesse's shoulder. Jesse tipped his hat and smiled down at the lady.

"Beg pardon, ma'am. Are you meaning to use the bank?"

"I certainly am," the lady replied, looking at the two men suspiciously.

"Well, ma'am, the thing is," Jesse stammered, "there's been a bit of an accident inside. My friend here took terrible sick in there a minute ago and well, I'm afraid he made a mess all over the floor.

And right by the front door, wouldn't you know. He's so embarrassed."

"Oh, dear," said the lady. "The poor man."

"We've got to run," said Jesse, moving past the woman. Bert staggered along beside him. "The manager's cleaning up that mess right now," Jesse said over his shoulder. "He's just locked the door for a few minutes. You know, the smell and all."

The lady made a face like she'd just stepped in something unpleasant. Her hand flew to her mouth.

Bert started to moan. "Let's goooooo," he seemed to say. When other strange sounds came from his throat, the lady stepped back a few paces.

"I can do my banking later," she said. "You get that poor man home. Or to a doctor. He looks dreadful."

"I'll do that ma'am," said Jesse. He dragged Bert to the Buick, helped him into the back seat, tossed the leather bag in behind him, jumped into the driver's seat and drove off in a cloud of dust. The lady stared after them, a puzzled look on her face. She could have sworn she heard the men laughing as the car turned onto the main road, going so fast that two of its wheels almost came right up off the ground.

The lady stood there for a moment or two, not knowing quite what to do next. She approached the front door of the bank, and peeked through the window. She looked down at the polished floor. Why,

Mr. Baldwin and his son have already got that mess cleaned up, she said to herself.

She rapped on the glass once, and then rapped again until her knuckles hurt. That's odd, she thought. They must be in there. Why don't they hear her?

Inside the vault, the banker heard someone knocking to get in. But he didn't get up.

"Dad! Who's that?" his son whispered.

"Don't know. Don't care," he whispered back.

"Shall I go see, Dad?"

"No. Stay put."

"Why?"

"Cause it hasn't been ten minutes yet, you fool."

Jesse and Bert had driven several miles down the road leading from Englehart to Haileybury when Bert chuckled and said, "That was so easy, Jesse. Whoop-dee-do! We're home free. And with a bundle of cash. Let's drive 100 miles or so, check in at a fancy hotel and have a blast."

"Not today, Bert," said Jesse. "You know our friend Mr. Baldwin will have called in an alarm by now. There'll be police in Haileybury and Cobalt looking for us. Here's the plan. Remember that little hide-away I told you about just north of Haileybury—the deserted miner's cabin deep in the woods? It's down a rough road that nobody ever drives over. We'll hide out there for a day or two, pretend we're a couple of hunters if anyone should stumble on us. We've got enough food and drink in the trunk to last us a week. When I figure it's safe, then we'll slip on down the highway, driving at night."

"Hey, sounds good to me," Bert grunted, fanning his face with his hat. "We can count our money at the cabin. And it'll be cooler in the woods than it is on this dusty road."

Within minutes, on the right hand side of the road, Jesse found the overgrown trail he was seeking and boldly turned the Buick into the woods. When the car was hidden from view by the dense growth, he stopped and got out.

"Hand me that broom in the back seat, Bert."

Bert reached back and found a long-handled broom. He tossed it out the open door to Jesse.

He watched as Jesse walked back to the main road and began to brush the loose sand back and forth, walking backwards, obliterating any tire tracks that might have been left by the car.

"Smart thinking, Jesse," Bert said approvingly when his accomplice climbed back in the driver's seat.

"I thought I saw some bicycle tracks," Jesse said thoughtfully. "But they could be old ones.

"How many sets?" asked Bert.

"Two sets, but the same tread. Chances are a guy

on a bike turned in here, saw how bumpy the trail was and headed back to the main road. Nobody's used this trail for years. And nobody remembers there's a cabin at the end of it."

He closed the car door and said, "Brace yourself, Bert. This is going to be a bumpy ride."

CHAPTER 7

SHOTS IN THE FOREST

School was cancelled in Haileybury for the rest of the week. Swirling clouds of smoke hung over the town and both the high school and public school principals sent their students home. Some students had complained of breathing problems and sore throats. No sooner had classes been dismissed than a light breeze swept in off the lake on two consecutive days, dispersing the smoke and allowing the sun to shine through.

Max and Marty decided to make use of their free time by bicycling north of town to one of their favourite spots—a trout stream known as Brooker's Creek. Their mother cautioned them when they left home. "You boys skedaddle right back here if there's any sign of dense smoke or fire." Amy trusted Max to do the sensible thing. "That boy is too good to be true," she had said to Harry more than once. "Marty's lucky to have him for a brother."

It was a bumpy road the boys followed from the main highway into the deep woods; a road filled with potholes and weeds, small rocks and loose sand. "This isn't a road, it's an obstacle course," Max shouted, weaving his bicycle around a large rock. The road led to Brooker's Creek where the brothers planned to do some fishing and exploring. Max had brought his geology book along and a small pickaxe. He wanted to chip away at some outcroppings. Perhaps someday he'd discover a rich vein of silver or gold.

"My bum is sore," Marty complained, wincing as his front wheel hit a rut, almost tossing him over the handlebars. "I won't be able to sit down for a month."

With Max leading the way, the boys pedalled hard up a steep incline and glided down the other side. "Hey, Marty, wasn't this a good idea?" Max called out. He was breathing hard. "It's a lot cooler here in the woods than it is in town."

"Better to be here than in math class," grunted Marty. "Yikes!" he shouted, twisting his handlebars to avoid another large rock. "I just hope there's some water left in the stream when we get there. Everything's so dry."

"There'll be plenty of water. It's a pretty big stream, remember. And there'll be a few small trout too, I bet. If we catch some we can cook 'em up right by the stream. If not, Mom packed us some tuna fish sandwiches."

"Yuck," Marty said, making a face. "Stinky old tuna fish. No peanut butter and jam?"

"No, Mom says there's too much sugar in jam. Besides, that's a kid's sandwich, good only at birthday parties."

"Says who?"

"Says me."

Marty snorted. "Every kid I know likes peanut butter and jam. And you like smelly tuna fish." He changed the subject. "After we go fishing, let's cool off with a swim," he suggested.

A few minutes later they heard the sounds of water falling over rocks. Their long ride—they were about four miles from town—was over. The boys dropped their bikes in a sandbank that lined Brooker's Creek. They placed a bottle of lemonade in the creek bed to chill it. They placed their backpacks on a rock next to their fishing rods, which they'd quickly assembled. Then they stripped off their shirts and flopped back in the hot sand. "This is a great place," Marty said, adjusting his folded shirt under his head. "Nobody ever comes here but us. It's our secret place. And the fishing and swimming's the best."

"Marty, I want to ask you something," Max said quietly. "And I hope you'll say it's okay."

Marty raised his head and frowned. "What is it? What's wrong?"

"Nothing's wrong. I just wondered how you'd feel if I told Sally about this place. And, you know, maybe even brought her here to see it. She's got a new bike and..."

"Oh, geez," Marty said, making a sour face. "Sally Logan. Not here. Not a girl. Oh, geez..."

There was a long silence. Max said calmly, "I was afraid you'd react like that. Obviously you don't like the idea. Come on, you know that Sally and I have been dating. Well, not exactly dating..."

"Is so dating! I call it dating."

"All right, then. We're dating," sighed Max.

"Right. You take a girl skating and to the movies. That's dating. Admit it."

"I did admit it. I think Sally's special, that's all. I like to be with her, so..."

"So you're dating. Big deal. Now you want to bring her here—to our special place. That's swell, Max. Why here? Girls hate fishing. You can't go skinny dipping with girls around. Girls can't stand sand in their shoes or ants in their pants. You ever see a girl bait a hook or clean a trout?"

"Okay, okay, I hear you," said Max.

"I can't believe you'd want to bring a girl out here," said Marty petulantly. He sat up and chewed on his lip. He stared at some birds drinking from the brook and tossed a pebble in their direction. They moved away but did not fly off. "What if Sally stepped on a garter snake or found a leech clinging to her leg? She'd faint I bet. After she screamed like a banshee."

"Sally's not like most girls," countered Max. "She can throw a baseball a ton and she runs and skates faster than most boys. A dog bit her once and she didn't even cry. And she's a bundle of fun. I've seen her bait a hook and if she found a snake out here she'd probably pick it up and hide it in your lunch pail."

Marty walked close to the stream and peered into a pool of deep water, looking for a school of trout. Nothing moved. Good, he thought, if you see them you could never catch them 'cause they can see you too.

Dern it all, he thought. *Why did this have to happen? Max likes Sally a lot, a whole lot. And I love my brother. But from now on it'll be more of Sally and Max and less of Marty and Max. Not much I can do about that. Sally's okay, a real good looker. Looks great in a sweater. But geez, whenever she wags her finger Max comes running like a fellow with his pants on fire. This is all part of growing up, I guess, but it seems pretty stupid to me. I don't like it and I don't really understand what I don't like about it.* He stood there for several seconds. Then he spit in the water, turned to his brother and said, "Hey, time for fishing."

They caught half a dozen small brook trout that day, using worms they found under rocks for bait. They slit open the plump white bellies of the trout with their sharp pocketknives, expertly gutted them, and popped out their eyes. "Yuck, I hate this part," said Marty, jumping back when an eyeball fell on his bare foot.

Max couldn't resist. "Wouldn't bother Sally," he teased. "She pops them out all the time."

"Liar," Marty said with a grin.

Max arranged a circular pile of rocks, found some kindling to put inside and struck a match. Soon he had a small blaze going. He pulled a frying pan from his pack, produced some flour and some butter and balanced the pan carefully on the rocks until the flames licked the underside. He plopped butter into the pan with his knife and sprinkled flour over the shiny trout. When the butter began to bubble and sizzle, he carefully placed the trout in the pan, and said, "Perfect."

Marty, meanwhile, was cutting thick slabs of bread with his knife and slapping butter on them. He withdrew some cheese from his pack, cut off a chunk for Max, and another for himself.

"The trout are almost done," Max said, turning one on its side with his knife, making sure the skin underneath was brown and crisp. "We'll have to eat them with our fingers. That's why I left the heads on. They're easier to handle that way."

"You finish cooking the fish while I fetch the lemonade."

"Dinner is served," announced Max, when his brother returned. Max gave Marty a peculiar look, cocked his head and said, "Listen."

The boys heard a strange sound in the woods, one that caused them to freeze in place. They stood still as a post, ignoring the simmering trout. They peered into the shadows that cloaked the woods.

"What the heck is making that noise?" Max asked, his voice little more than a whisper.

"Darned if I know," Marty answered. "Sounds like an engine."

"It is an engine—a car engine," Max said. "But it can't be. You saw the road, all ruts and rocks. How could a car possibly get this deep in the woods?"

"I don't know," Marty replied. "Maybe we should just scram out of here."

"No," said Max. "Let's go take a look. Won't take a minute. We'll come right back for the trout."

"What about the fire? Shouldn't we put it out?"

Max hesitated. He looked down at the smoldering fire. It looked harmless. "No, we'll do it when we get back. It's mostly embers anyway. And we'll only be gone a few minutes."

The two boys slipped into the woods and followed a path that led to the bumpy road. Marty pointed at the ground. "Those are tire tracks," he said. "Somebody just passed by here in a car."

"That's really odd," said Max. "Let's follow the tracks. There's something funny going on here."

They followed the tracks for a couple of hundred yards until they came to a clearing in the woods.

"Look! There's a log shack," Marty exclaimed. "And there's a car hidden in behind it. Looks like a yellow one. You can barely see it."

"I think it's a deserted prospector's cabin," Max said, pulling back a branch for a closer look. "If we hadn't heard the car engine we'd never have known there was a cabin back here."

"Let's go see if there's someone inside," Marty suggested. "Might be hunters in there. Maybe it's even someone we know."

"No, something tells me we should wait here for a few minutes. Stay out of sight and see what happens." The brothers slipped deeper into the woods.

They could hear voices coming from the shack and then the front door flew open. A man appeared carrying something in one hand. It looked like a container or small bag of some sort—perhaps a saddlebag.

"Do you recognize him?" whispered Marty.

"Can't tell. It's a long way to the shack. One of them looks familiar but I can't recall where I've seen him before. I'd have to get closer."

"What are they doing?"

"One of them just sat down on the grass. He's opening the sack and taking something out. Now he's laughing. Can you hear him?"

"Yeah, I hear him. What about the other guy?"

"Now he's coming out the door. Uh oh, he's carrying a rifle. Don't let them see us. Stay down."

Max took a peek through the branches and saw the man with the rifle move a few steps in their direction. Then he stopped and stared straight at their hiding place, as if he'd spotted them. Max felt a small chill go up his spine. The man began to raise his rifle. Unbeknownst to the boys, a rabbit had hopped from the nearby woods and stood nibbling on some tender shoots. The rabbit hopped to a spot directly between the boys and the man with the rifle. The man drew a bead and fired off a round.

CRACK!

The rifle shot echoed through the woods and a bullet screamed past the boys' feet, slapping into a tree trunk. Max and Marty jumped, falling into each other.

"My gosh, he's seen us," said Marty, his voice trembling with fear. "He's trying to kill us."

"Be quiet!" ordered Max, trying to control his own anxiety. "Let's get out of here. Follow me. Be fast and be quiet." The boys turned and dashed deeper into the woods.

CRACK!

A second shot ripped through the leaves behind them and convinced them to run even faster. Branches lashed their faces and they stumbled over roots in their haste to escape the madman with the gun. Soon they were hopelessly lost. When they heard no more shots and felt they were reasonably safe, the boys fell to the ground and caught their breath. Marty complained of a stitch in his side.

"Geez, Max, we're in real trouble now. These woods go on for miles. What are we going to do? And why was that old coot shooting at us?"

"I don't know, Marty. Haven't a clue. But listen to me. The thing is, we can't panic, okay? I believe we'll find our way back to the old road if we walk in this direction." Max pointed to his right. "I tried to keep some sense of direction when we were running but I may be wrong. I'm going by my instincts. You want to trust them?"

"I sure don't trust my own," answered Marty, jumping up. "We better get going. The sooner we get our bikes and get out of here, the better."

Max put a hand on his brother's shoulder. "Marty, we can't go back to Brooker's Creek even if we do find the road again. Not now. It's too close to that old shack and the crazy man with the rifle. I think we should walk home—if we find the road—and come back tomorrow for the bikes and anything else we left by the stream. Okay?"

"A deal," said Marty, even though the idea of walking all the way home didn't really appeal to him. Still, it was better than being shot at by a madman.

It took the boys two hours to find the old road. To keep moving in a straight line, Max insisted on blazing the trunks of trees with his pocketknife. Otherwise they might have wound up walking in circles and being stranded for days. They breathed a sigh of relief when they stumbled out of the dense bush and made their way back onto the rutted road. "That was a close call," said Max, sitting on a stump to rest. "Get lost in there and your chances of survival are really slim."

"Now we've got to walk all the way home," sighed Marty, flopping on the grass and scratching at a bite. "We've lost our bikes, our lemonade and our fish dinner. My feet hurt, I'm bitten by bugs, covered with burrs and I've got the sorest bum in the whole wide world. Remember I fell off that stupid ladder and that bicycle seat of mine didn't help any."

"Listen, I know it's not pleasant," replied Max, sounding annoyed. "But you're alive, little brother. And you might not be if that gunman was more of a sharpshooter."

"You're right about that, Max. Which reminds me. That car we saw in the clearing might come bouncing back down this road any minute. So let's keep our feet moving. I don't ever want to meet those guys again—not unless I've got a machine gun and a barrel of bullets."

Max hauled his brother up by the arm. "Back to Haileybury," he said. "And not a word to anyone about what happened today. Mom and Dad will only worry. Let's hope those men will be gone when we come back tomorrow. And let's hope they didn't find our bikes and steal them. If Mom finds out someone was shooting at us, she'll never let us come back to Brooker's Creek again."

CHAPTER 8
FIRE SWEEPS THROUGH TOWN

"Well, boys, how was the fishing trip?" Mrs. Mitchell asked as she placed plates of steaming spaghetti and meat sauce in front of them.

"It was okay," said Marty, reaching for a slice of his mom's fresh-baked bread. "We caught some trout and Max cooked them up over a campfire." He neglected to mention that they hadn't eaten the trout but had left them sizzling in a frying pan.

"I hope you doused that fire with plenty of water before you left," Mrs. Mitchell said, "like your father taught you."

"Hmmm," murmured Max, his mouth full of spaghetti. He swallowed, then yelped, creating a distraction. "This sauce is too hot, Mom." He waved a hand in front of his mouth, grabbed for a glass of milk and gulped it down. He smacked his lips.

"That's better. Say, that's great tasting milk, Mom."

His mother gave him a puzzled look. "Milk is milk, son. It always tastes the same."

"No, Mom, it always tastes better after a day in the woods. Much better."

"Then I'll get you some more," she said. She picked up his empty glass and went to the icebox.

The brothers grinned at each other, knowing they'd successfully turned the conversation away from their fishing trip.

"Mom, where's Dad tonight?" Marty asked when she came back. "Is he working late again?"

"He's at the paper filing a report. He got a call from the *New York Times* today. An editor there wants him to file some stories about the forest fires raging out of control in the North Country. Then he has to write a local story—about the big bank robbery today in Englehart. Writing for the *New York Times* is quite an honour. Your father has been promised a byline and some extra money."

"Gee, that's great," said Max. "About time someone recognized Dad's talents as a writer."

"Somebody robbed a bank?" asked Marty.

"Indeed they did. Two robbers with a gun walked off with all the money in the Englehart bank. I'm afraid the North Country's getting to be more and more like a big city when it comes to crime."

"I guess Dad will mention the big fire that's burning up the bush west of here," Max said.

"I'm sure he will, Max. Let's just pray the men fighting the fire don't get hurt. Perhaps it'll rain soon and they'll be able to get it under control."

"That fire must be getting pretty darn close to us," Marty said, dipping a crust of bread into the sauce on his plate. "Max and I could smell a lot of smoke when we were fishing today."

Max glared at his brother, as if to say, *Stop talking about fishing, you goofball.*

"I feel sorry for anyone living in the path of a forest fire," Mrs. Mitchell sighed as she sat down to eat. "I'm sure I've told you how my folks lost everything to a fire when I was a young girl. The farm, the cattle, everything gone in a matter of minutes. My folks threw everything of value into a wagon, my dad hitched up Horace and Maude and those poor horses galloped for about ten miles before we felt safe. If we'd broken an axle or a wheel, we'd never have made it. The fire was that close. We were frightened to death. My dad never went back. He moved us all to Haileybury after that."

Marty hadn't heard the story. "We're not in any danger of being burned out here, are we Mom?" he asked.

"I don't think so, son. We should be safe in Haileybury unless the wind picks up and turns the fire in this direction. That's not likely to happen. But then, it's not a precise science, predicting what

Mother Nature is likely to do. She's got a bagful of tricks, like fires and floods and earthquakes. And she can make life miserable for folks when she has a mind to."

"I'd feel a lot safer if I knew the Dooley brothers had finished their work on the firebreak," Max said. "They're such slowpokes. Can you believe they took a couple of days off to go hunting?"

Hours later, in the middle of the night, Max was awakened from a sound sleep by the clanging of a bell. He rolled out of bed and ran to the window. He raised the blind, looked out and saw dark figures scurrying along Marcella Street. Max opened the window and leaned out. The air was thick with smoke. In the street below, a man holding a cowbell was ringing it loudly. Another man—it looked like the fire chief—was pounding on doors, waking the sleeping residents inside. The man with the bell looked up and saw Max. "Get everybody up, son!" he shouted. "Fire's coming! Leave everything and run for your lives!"

For a moment or two, Max was stunned, too surprised to move. Behind him he heard Marty scrambling out of bed. Across the street, old Mrs. Lewis, a widow, ran from her house carrying a shovel. She held a small box under her other arm. She ran to her garden and frantically began digging.

"Mom! Dad! Get up!" Max shouted down the hall.

He started to throw on his clothes.

He glanced out the window and saw Mrs. Lewis bury the box in the hole she'd dug. She dashed back inside, and reappeared almost instantly, wearing her fur coat—her most prized possession. Then she trotted off down the middle of the street. Her nightgown showed beneath her coat and she was wearing pink bedroom slippers. She lost both of her slippers before she'd covered half a block.

In the distance, over the roofs of the houses, Max could see flashes of red and orange and yellow. Flames! Giant flames! A gust of wind fanned his face. The wind must have changed and was bringing the flames to Haileybury. Max could hear the wind whistling through the branches of the huge pine tree on the corner and rattling the loose slats on Mrs. Lewis' fence. Sparks danced through the air and one or two landed on the roof of the Lewis bungalow.

Max ducked back into the bedroom, closing the window, shutting out the wind and the smoke. Marty was dancing on one foot, pulling on a pant leg.

"Max, what's happening out there?" Marty croaked.

"Hurry! Get dressed!" ordered Max. He ran down the hall and pounded on the door to his parents' room. "Mom! Dad! Get up. We've got to get out of here. The wind's changed and there's a monster fire headed this way."

The bedroom door flew open. "We heard, son. We're almost dressed. Go to the kitchen. You and Marty fill some bottles with tap water. I'll get the strongbox from my office."

Max had the presence of mind to grab a pair of sturdy boots. "Wear your boots," he told Marty. "We might need them before the day is over."

Marty was fumbling with the buttons on his shirt. "Didn't they say the fire wouldn't come this way?" he said, alarmed. "Didn't they say the fire couldn't reach the town?"

"That was yesterday," answered Max tersely, lacing up a boot. "And obviously they were wrong."

The boys raced downstairs, filled four bottles full of water and capped the bottles tightly. Mr. Mitchell went to his office and returned carrying the strongbox. The box contained some important papers, some cash, an ancient gold watch and some rare coins he'd collected over the years. Mrs. Mitchell flew down the stairs and placed her jewellery and some family photos she treasured in the box. "That's it," she said grimly, closing the box and locking it.

"I'll carry the box to the car," Marty volunteered.

"No, we're not taking it with us," said Mr. Mitchell. "We may have to pick up people who don't have cars and drive them to safety. Or we may have to abandon the car and run for the lake. We'll bury the box in the back yard. It'll be safe under the ground. Marty, fetch a spade from the shed."

Marty found two spades. He and Max quickly dug a deep hole in the soft earth of the garden. "There go Mom's potato plants," Marty grunted.

"Can't be helped," answered Max. "Besides, they may be baked potatoes before long."

Together the boys slipped the metal box into the hole and covered it over. Max marked the spot with a large stone.

"If the house burns down, we'll come back for the box," he said. "People in town without transportation will be doing the same thing—like Mrs. Lewis."

"What's next, Dad?" Marty shouted at his father who stood at the back door. The window next to his father appeared to be ablaze. Then Marty realized it was merely a reflection of flames devouring the nearby woods.

"Quick! Get in the car!" Mr. Mitchell shouted. "I've got the water bottles and some food in a bag. Run for it!"

The family car, an old Durant Mr. Mitchell had purchased second-hand for 100 dollars, was parked next to the house. Max had learned how to drive it. He washed it once a week and polished the chrome. Marty couldn't wait until he was 16 and it was his turn. The Mitchells leaped into the vehicle and slammed the doors.

"Holy cow!" yelled Marty, peering through the windshield. "The whole stinking street's on fire. Get this old heap moving, Dad."

Mr. Mitchell pumped the gas pedal and turned the key. The Durant's motor made a whirring noise. Then it stopped. He tried again. Grrrr-uppp. Grrr-uppp.

"Geez, Dad," Marty said in alarm. "Won't she start?"

"Maybe you flooded it," Max suggested.

"You filled the gas tank, didn't you Harry?" Mrs. Mitchell said nervously.

"Let me try it, Dad," said Max, jumping out of the back seat and into the front, pushing his father almost into his mother's lap.

Max took the wheel, waited a few seconds, and then turned the key.

Rummmmmmm, Rmmmmmmmm. The engine caught.

Marty cheered. "Gun it, Max!" he shouted.

The car leaped forward, almost striking a clump of birch trees next to the driveway. Max made a sharp right turn onto Marcella Street and raced toward the centre of town. A few hundred yards behind them, in the dust thrown up by the spinning tires, there was fire everywhere. And noise. The Mitchells heard a "WHOOF" over the roar of the car engine as a flaming tree crashed onto the roof of the McCowan house. Next to the McCowan place, the LeClair's barn was ablaze. Cattle could be heard bawling in the field. Two dogs, barking and snapping at each other, ran into the street and Max swerved to avoid hitting them. Half a dozen terrified deer leaped over a burning fence and huddled in the ditch beside the road, not knowing which way to turn. "Poor souls," murmured Mrs. Mitchell.

A line of cars careened down the street ahead of them. Some had passengers riding on the running boards. A man on a motorcycle, with two bulging saddlebags and a female passenger clinging to his waist, raced past the Mitchell's car. The man tried to avoid a pothole and his machine veered to the right and skidded out of control. The motorcycle slammed into the ditch, throwing its driver and his screaming passenger into some high grass.

"Are they hurt?" Marty shouted from the back seat.

"I think they're okay," said Max.

Marty turned to look out the back window. "They're up and running—like everybody else. Someone pulled over to pick them up."

The Mitchells passed people carrying satchels and suitcases. Some were pushing baby carriages. Others pulled children in small wagons. Frightened youngsters holding the hands of parents and older siblings clung tightly to dolls and stuffed animals. Others carried kittens and small dogs. An elderly couple holding wet towels to their faces came into view.

"Stop the car, Max!" ordered Mr. Mitchell. "It's old Mr. Callahan and his wife Lizzie. He's getting over a stroke and she's got a bad hip. Get them in with us."

Max didn't hesitate. He flew out of the car, took the Callahans by the arm, and ushered them into the back seat next to Marty. The old couple they'd rescued, gasping and coughing, voiced their thanks. Mr. Callahan put his bald head back. His wife wiped his brow with the damp cloth.

"This can't be the big fire that was burning to the west of Haileybury," Mr. Mitchell said. "That fire couldn't possibly have reached us this quickly. This fire must have been started locally. Probably some dern fool being careless with matches or someone throwing a cigarette from a car. City people, probably." There was disgust in his voice. "Now we're going to lose the whole town because of somebody's stupidity."

Max gripped the wheel tightly. There was a sudden sinking feeling in his stomach. A local fire, his father had said. Someone careless with matches. He thought of the fishing hole and the small fire he'd started—and hadn't taken the time to put out. A horrible thought crossed his mind: *What if it's my fault?*

"Dad, I've got to get out." He pulled the car to the curb. "You take the wheel."

"What is it, Max?" his mother asked.

"It's Sally Logan and her family. They live on a back road about a half-mile from here. Their house is isolated. What if they're still asleep? They'll be burned in their beds. I should have phoned."

"The lines are probably down," Mr. Mitchell said.

"Somebody has to warn the Logans."

"I'll go with you, Max," Marty volunteered, scrambling out of the back seat.

"Max! Marty! Please don't go!" their mother cried out. But the doors had slammed shut.

Max had already started trotting down the side road. He shouted back over his shoulder, "You and Mom drive to Cobalt. The wind isn't headed in that direction. Marty and I will go and make sure the Logans are safe. We'll meet you in Cobalt in an hour or so."

"It's five miles to Cobalt!" called Mr. Mitchell. "You can't walk there. It's too dangerous."

"Dad, there's our motorboat. The fire hasn't reached the lake yet. We'll go to Cobalt by boat. But first I've got to check on the Logans. They may be in real danger."

Before their parents could put up any further argument, Max and Marty started running along the road toward the Logan's. Suddenly, Max called Marty to a halt.

"I've been thinking..."

"About what?" Marty was almost breathless.

"About yesterday..." Max looked frightened. Marty had never seen that look in his brother's eyes and it frightened him, too.

"You mean the fishing trip?" said Marty. "Leaving our bikes, that crazy man shooting at us?"

"Yeah, and the fire I started. What if...?"

Marty nodded. "I was thinking it too."

"Marty, this is really serious. It may be my fault the town is burning down. It was probably the stupidest thing I've ever done. Now look what's happened. People may die. I could go to jail."

"I'm not going to tell, Max. And it was partly my fault, too."

Max angrily shook his head. "No, no, I'm to blame. It was my decision. I started the fire and I should have put it out. I should have known better." He smiled wanly. "But thanks, anyway. We better keep moving."

"Look! There's Sally's house," cried Marty. He grabbed Max by the arm and pointed. "Wow! Look at the flames in those fields next to it."

They sprinted up to the Logan's front door and Max pounded on it. "Anybody home?" he shouted. "Mr. Logan! Sally!"

Within seconds a light came on inside. "What in tarnation!" exclaimed Mr. Logan, throwing open the door. He gasped when he saw a sheet of flame lighting up the nearby field.

"Get everybody up!" cried Max. "The whole town is burning."

Sally appeared in the doorway wearing a blue house-coat over her nightgown. "What's happening, Max?"

"Sally, get dressed," ordered Max. "Wake your brothers and sisters. Get them out of the house—now!"

"You can bury your valuables in a box or a trunk," Marty added.

"There's a shovel and a spade in the barn," Sally said, dashing back into the house.

While the Logans scurried around inside the house, Max and Marty ran to the barn, found the tools, and began digging a hole in the soft ground of the garden. While they dug, fire swept across the grass of the nearby pasture. Burning branches snapped and crackled in the woods behind the barn. The noise was deafening.

Mr. Logan and Sally burst from the house lugging a huge trunk. Then came Mrs. Logan dragging four-year-old Billy. The Logan twins—a boy and a girl—followed.

"Put the trunk here!" shouted Max.

"Can't we throw it in the back of the truck?" Sally asked.

"No! We need room for the kids," grunted Mr. Logan. "We may have to pick up some people along the way. It'll be safe here, buried in the ground."

Hastily, Max and Marty buried the trunk. Mr. Logan picked up a large rock and settled it on the dirt to mark the spot.

Everybody raced to the truck, which was parked nearby. Whoosh! A wall of flame shot up from behind the house, leaving it in silhouette.

"Look out, everybody!" cried Sally. The roof of the hen house exploded in flames and a dozen terrified squawking chickens raced in all directions.

"C'mon!" shouted Mr. Logan, calling through his cupped hands. "Get in the truck!"

The Logans hurried to the old pickup and leaped aboard.

"Come on, Max! Come on, Marty!" Sally shrieked.

Just then, Billy Logan turned from the truck and darted back toward the house.

"Sparky!" whined Billy. "Where's Sparky?"

Billy scurried through the open door and disappeared into the smoke-filled hall.

"Billy!" screamed Mrs. Logan. "Billy! Come back here!"

"He's gone after Sparky!" Sally shouted. "I'll go get him."

"No, you won't," Max said firmly. "I'll do it."

Max raced into the house. Inside the front door he could hear Billy crying and the whimpering of a dog. Max crouched low to the floor, holding his breath to avoid the choking smoke. His eyes stung mercilessly. "Billy!" he shouted. The smoke slammed into his throat like a balled fist. He almost fell over Billy, who was down on his knees, coughing and crying. At Billy's feet, a small dog lay shaking with fear.

Max scooped child and dog up in his arms, turned and staggered outside.

"Billy!" cried Mrs. Logan. "Oh, Billy." She took her son from Max and the lad buried his grime-covered face in her shoulder.

Mrs. Logan flung her other arm around Max and squeezed hard. "Thank you, Max," she whispered before climbing into the cab.

"Let's go, let's go!" cried Mr. Logan, revving the motor. In his rear-view mirror he could see his house being swallowed in flames. A burning shingle cartwheeled through the air and landed on the hood of his truck, creating a shower of sparks. Another flew past his open window. "Hold on!" He stepped hard on the accelerator.

The truck bounced along the dirt road leading toward the main road. Max lay down on the truck bed and inhaled deeply. He put one arm across his forehead. He was dizzy from the smoke. He wanted to clear his lungs. Tears spilled from his sore eyes.

"Max," said Sally. "What's the matter?"

Max tried to choke back the words but he couldn't. He told her about the campfire and how guilty he felt. He turned his head away, not wanting her to see his tears.

"Oh, no," she said. "My poor Max."

When their old truck reached the main road leading to Cobalt, the Logans found themselves in the midst of a huge caravan of cars, trucks, horse-drawn wagons, tractors and bicycles. The road was crowded with people, an exodus of refugees forced from their warm beds in the middle of the night.

By then, Max was standing in the back of the truck, his sore eyes dry and wide. One arm was slung around his brother. He held Sally by the hand. What he was seeing sickened him. He recalled a newsreel he'd seen at the Bijou months before. He'd been saddened by a few fleeting seconds of images that had flashed on the screen, images from some war-ravaged European nation he'd never heard of, a film of refugees wearing ragged clothes fleeing from some cruel dictator whose name he couldn't pronounce or even remember. The poor homeless people on the Bijou's screen pulled small carts with big wobbly wheels—carts piled high with their worldly goods. As they passed the cameraman, their faces, full of despair, devoid of hope, lined with worry, were caught in his lens.

Max thought of those images now. In mute horror he watched as hundreds of Haileyburians marched along the road, carrying all that was left of their lives. Everything else destroyed. Their homes, their schools, their churches. Gone.

He was thinking, *It's all my fault.*

CHAPTER 9
THE YOUNG LIFESAVERS

The truck slowed to a crawl. The entire town must be on this road, thought Max miserably. Wait until they find out what I've done.

"Tell your folks we're going to the lake," Max called to Sally as he and Marty jumped off the back. "Tell them not to worry. The worst of the fire is to the north of us. It hasn't reached the beach down this way—not yet. We'll save our outboard and get to Cobalt by following the shoreline..."

"Wait! I'm coming with you," Sally called back. "Catch me, Max!" She leaped from the truck into Max's arms. He held her for a moment, and then looked straight into her blue eyes. "You'd better be able to keep up, Sally," he warned her.

She frowned and tossed her curls. "I'll keep up. Don't worry about me."

"Let's go, then." The three teens darted down a side street leading to Lake Temiskaming.

"Look!" cried Sally. "The lake is full of people."

Hundreds of Haileyburians were huddled together, standing waist-deep in the water. Whipped by the hot winds generated by the fire, flames had closed in around the beach. And around them. Those who had tried to escape along the shoreline in either direction had been forced to turn back. They were trapped. They waded into the lake.

Flames from burning storage sheds lining part of the sandy beach shot a hundred feet in the air, throwing sparks and embers in all directions. Picnic tables on the beach were ablaze. One had toppled over onto the turrets of a child's abandoned sandcastle.

Far out in the shallow water, adults held young children in their arms, shielding their small bodies and frightened faces from the raging fire on shore. Every few seconds, heads ducked below the surface, only to reappear slick and shining and cooler. The reflection from the flames danced along the crest of the waves and lit up the agonized faces. They looked like ghoulish devil masks.

Some brave men tried to halt the approaching inferno. They rigged horses to wagons and dashed along the shore. The frightened animals whinnied and snorted and rolled their big eyes. The drivers pulled hard on the reins, leaped off the carts and began filling empty barrels with water from the lake.

The men, straining and grunting under the weight of the barrels, hauled them back onto the wagons. They jumped aboard. "Gid-yep!" and "Go, hoss, go!" they cried as they cracked their whips. The horses reluctantly but obediently turned and started back toward the fire line where men with sooty faces dumped the barrels in what was a futile attempt to hold back the roaring flames.

The lucky few who owned boats made their way to the middle of the lake where they bobbed at anchor. Most boat owners had stopped to pluck friends and neighbors from the cold, choppy water, hauling people aboard until their boat threatened to capsize and go under. Others, thinking only of themselves, ignored all pleas for help.

"Over there!" shouted Max, pointing. A man lay unconscious in the sand. He had tried to steal a canoe. Two other men had pounced on him and beat him with paddles and fists.

Scores of people had sought refuge on the long wharf that jutted out into the lake but they found no safety.

"Jump!" shouted Max. "You have no choice."

The teens watched in helpless horror as the flames rolled along the dock. Suddenly they could hear splashing sounds. Dozens of frightened people were leaping into the water. Their screams filled the air.

Someone shouted at the top of his lungs, "Run for

it! They're going to blow!" He was pointing at a dozen red gasoline drums standing on the dock. Suddenly a series of violent explosions rocked the area. Booom! Boom! Sheets of flame lit up the sky and the ground shook from the awesome blasts. Dock timbers, each weighing 100 pounds or more, were hurled in the air, then slammed back into the dock or into the water. The crashing, splintering, splashing sounds, and the awesome roar of the advancing fire created more panic. People seeking refuge on the dock fled in terror, their hands over their ears, hurrying to the very end of the wharf. They cringed in fear as the flames raced swiftly toward them. When the fire drew unbearably close, they were forced to leap feet first into the frigid water. They swam away from the dock, then turned and struck out awkwardly toward the shore, a distance of several hundred feet. "Oh, no," moaned Sally. Two elderly swimmers, their clothes dragging them down, succumbed quickly and slipped silently below the surface. Others struggled on, sobbing and gasping for breath, until they could touch bottom, until they could reach out to those standing in the shallows and be pulled into the group.

"Let's get to our boat!" cried Marty. "We've got to get out of here."

Max, Marty and Sally dashed along the beach toward the boathouse, which was several hundred yards downwind from the flames.

Marty pointed a finger. "Look! The door's wide open!"

They rushed through the open door into the boat-house. "Somebody's been in here," Max said, "The lock is broken. And our boat is gone. Somebody's stolen it."

Sally gripped Max by the wrist. "Listen," she said, "Hear that? Someone's trying to start an outboard motor. And they're not far away."

"Right, Sally. And they're having trouble starting it."

They ran back outside.

"There it is, Max. The Queen Vic. Our boat." Marty was pointing down the beach. "And there's someone in it."

Max cupped his hands and shouted. "Hey, you! What are you doing in our boat?"

A pair of dark figures standing in the boat turned in their direction.

"Come on. Let's go after them," Max cried.

The three teens ran toward the boat, which was now drifting slowly away from the shore. One of the dark figures aboard the craft dropped the motor's starting cord, leaped into the shallow water and scurried away, his partner at his heels. They darted into the nearby woods and disappeared.

"Stop, you thieves!" yelled Sally. But of course the men didn't stop. They vanished.

The Mitchell's boat, meanwhile, was drifting into deeper water. Max dashed into the lake after it, and with the water almost up to his shoulders, managed to grab a rope trailing from the bow. Digging his heels into the sandy bottom, he was able to drag the boat to shore. Marty and Sally helped him pull the craft onto the beach.

"That was close," Marty said. "I thought the old Queen Vic was a goner. I wonder who those rotten thieves were?"

"I think I know who they were," said Max grimly, as he examined the boat's motor. "They may have been those men at Brooker's Creek, the guys who took a couple of shots at us."

"Somebody shot at you?" Sally gasped.

Max said, "I'll tell you all about it later, Sally. Right now this motor needs gas. Marty, run back to the boathouse, will you? Bring us back a can of gasoline."

"Now we know why the thief couldn't start it," laughed Marty. "The tank was empty. What a dummy!" Max turned and gave his brother a look. "Okay, I'm going," Marty said. "I'll be back in a flash—and with some gas."

A few minutes later, with a full tank of gas, the boat and its three young occupants roared away from the shore.

"Now we're off to Cobalt," Marty shouted, the

wind ruffling his hair.

"Not so fast," replied Max, suddenly making a sharp turn. "Look! There are people in the water over there. We can't leave them to drown."

Within seconds, the Queen Vic was circling the swimmers, its motor idling. Max, Marty and Sally began pulling four exhausted swimmers into the boat. Most were so cold they could barely speak. One little red-haired boy was unconscious. Max rolled him over, hoping to clear his lungs of water. Then began breathing into the lad's open mouth. That did it. The boy blinked his eyes and began coughing up copious amounts of lake water. He began to cry. Sally put her arm around him and tried to comfort him.

"He's frightened but I think he'll be all right," Max said grimly. He gunned the motor and turned the boat toward the boathouse.

"Stop the boat, Max!" Sally screamed. "There's a woman in the water just ahead. She's drowning!"

Max cut the motor. A few feet away a young woman was desperately trying to keep her head above the waves. Then she tired and disappeared.

Max took a deep breath and dove in after her. Beneath the surface, he groped wildly in several directions. Nothing. Then he felt something brush his arm and he reached out. He caught his hand in her long hair. He gripped tightly and pushed to the surface. He came up gasping, his lungs on fire. He pulled the woman's head above the chop and cupped her chin with one hand. With Marty's help, he was able to ease the exhausted woman into the boat. They had to be careful because the boat was now riding low in the water and was in danger of capsizing. The young woman clung to Max while Marty moved to the stern and re-started the motor.

"Why, it's Agnes Witherspoon!" Sally gasped. Agnes was one of her best friends. They were in the same class at school.

Agnes coughed several times, and then sucked in fresh air, taking deep breaths. She tried to stand but lost her balance and fell toward Max who grabbed her in both arms. Her face close to his, Agnes murmured, "Thank you, Max. You just saved my life." She sat down next to Max, then turned and gave Sally a weak smile. "What a horrible night, Sal," she sighed. "I was alone at home when the fire swept down our street. It was so sudden. My parents are in Cobalt, visiting friends. I had to run for my life—to the lake. Got out over my head..." Her voice trailed off, her eyes closed and she fell back again. Luckily, Max caught her and lowered her into the boat.

"She's fainted, Sally," Max shouted over the roar of the outboard. "Let's move these people up to the Cobalt road. Somebody will help us there. Maybe there's a trolley still running. I'm afraid the Queen

Vic will capsize if we try to get to Cobalt by boat."

Expertly, Marty steered the boat to shore and beached her. He and Sally helped the people they'd rescued out of the boat. Then Marty pulled the Queen Vic higher up on the beach. Agnes was awake, but complained of a headache. "Will you carry me, Max?" she pleaded.

"Agnes," he said, "you look strong enough to make it on your own. I'm more concerned about the boy here." Agnes pouted as Max swept the boy into his arms. "I'll carry you, bud," he said. "You're a little too weak to walk. Everybody follow me. I don't want anybody wandering away."

He struck out along the beach, leading the small group of survivors along a trail and then up a hill to the Haileybury-Cobalt road. Next to the road were the trolley tracks. A trolley was approaching. Max lowered the boy onto some soft grass. He stood in the middle of the tracks, waving his arms. Max saw Wendel Wilkins, the veteran trolley man, reach for his bell. He clanged it several times. The message was clear: *Get out of my way!* Max didn't flinch. At the last second Wilkins hit the brakes. The trolley screeched to a shuddering halt. Wilkins threw open the door, leaned out and shouted, "Step aside, boy! There's no more room aboard."

"Then we'll make room," Max answered boldly. "These people have been in the lake and they need medical attention." He lifted the boy to a tall man inside the trolley and ushered the others into the car. People had to squeeze together to make room.

"You climb aboard too, Sally," he ordered. "Look after these folks when you get to Cobalt. Make sure Agnes finds her parents. Marty and I will follow along. We'll see you soon." Suddenly he was gone. The doors closed and the trolley heaved slowly forward. Through the window, Sally looked at Max and managed a sweet smile. He grinned back at her and waved.

Max felt a tug on his sleeve. "Let's get going," said Marty. "This is a nightmare."

Back on the trolley, Wilkins was grumbling. "Shouldn't have stopped back there," he complained loudly. "That nervy young fella made me do it. Wouldn't listen. Now I'll be lucky to reach Cobalt before the power goes off. Could happen any second. Then we'll all have to walk. And it'll be his fault, not mine."

Agnes and Sally were huddled close together behind the driver.

"You really like him, don't you?" Agnes whispered in Sally's ear. Sally turned and almost bumped noses with her friend. "Of course I do. Everybody likes Max. Just between us, Ag, I think he's amazing," Sally confided. "So brave and decisive. Not like some of those immature kids at school."

"You make him sound so perfect," Agnes snorted sourly. "Nobody's perfect. Personally, I think he could be a lot more considerate." Agnes was still angry with Max because he had refused to carry her from the boat. And she was furious with his kid brother Marty too. She had overheard Marty say, "Carry her, Max? She must weigh a ton."

Sally frowned, hurt by her friend's nasty tone. "Oh, I know Max isn't perfect. Not all the time."

The truth was Agnes had a long-standing crush on Max—until tonight. Now she felt spurned. She was mad as a toad poked with a stick when she realized that Max had eyes only for Sally.

"Tell me one thing about Max that's not perfect, Sal? There must be something."

"Can you keep a secret?"

"Of course."

"Max thinks he may be responsible for tonight's fire. He left a campfire burning at Brooker's Creek and it may have flared up. He's sick with guilt."

"How awful!" said Agnes. "If people find out they'll despise him. They'll want him jailed or run out of town. Poor Max."

"Hush, not so loud," Sally said. She saw the trolley man looking in their direction. Poor Max, indeed, thought Agnes. It wouldn't hurt for him to be taken down a peg or two. Perhaps if Sally found out Max was reviled by everyone in the community she wouldn't want him any more.

A few minutes later, the trolley car screeched to a stop in Cobalt.

"That does it," muttered Wilkins. "The trolley line is now out of commission. Follow me, folks. Take your belongings. Everybody is seeking shelter in the town hall."

CHAPTER 10
THE SURVIVORS REACH COBALT

Max watched the trolley disappear into the night when he felt another tug on his sleeve. "Now let's get back to the boat and head for Cobalt," said Marty. The air was thick with smoke. To the west, Marty saw flames shooting up 100 feet in the air. It looked like the sky was on fire. "Let's go, Max. Our folks are going to be worried sick. Things are getting too dern hot around here."

Max was about to agree when he saw some people running down the road toward them. He recognized Dr. Gamble, the town's only surgeon. Three nurses hurried to keep up with him.

"Will there be any more trolleys, son?" the doctor asked.

"I don't know, sir," Max replied. "I don't think so. We just put some people on the last one."

"Then we'll have to walk to Cobalt," the doctor said to the nurses.

"Fine with us," answered one of the nurses. Max recognized her as Miss Wilson. The Wilsons lived near the Mitchells, two streets over.

Miss Wilson came forward, a strained look on her face. "You're the Mitchell boys, aren't you? Oh, I have such terrible news. It's about your friend Benjie—Benjie McNab."

"What happened to Benjie?" Max exclaimed. Benjie was one of his best pals, a star defenceman on the hockey team. Max knew Benjie was in the hospital with a bad case of stomach cramps.

"Swollen appendix," said Dr. Gamble. "We were about to operate. Your friend had even been anesthetized. We had no idea the fire was so close. Then all the lights went out. The alarm went off. We were ordered to evacuate the hospital. In the confusion, Benjie disappeared. Somehow he was left behind." Miss Wilson began to sob.

Max was shocked and angry. He couldn't believe what he'd heard. "How could you leave him behind?" he demanded.

"We all thought the orderlies took him away," Miss Wilson replied, her voice rising and the tears spilling down her cheeks. "But when we got outside, Benjie was missing. By then the hospital was ablaze. There was so much smoke and confusion." Her voice broke and she dabbed once more at her eyes.

Max didn't want to hear any more. His lips

tightened and he turned to Marty. "Let's go back."

"Go back?" Marty was startled. "To the boat?"

"No! To the hospital. To look for Benjie. Nobody seems to care whether he lives or dies. Except us. We're his friends."

"It's no use," cried Miss Wilson. "It's too dangerous. And probably too late. Please don't go back. You'll both be burned to death."

But Max was already on the run, Marty shrugged. He had no choice but to follow. Whenever Max decided on a plan of action, Marty always supported him. No matter what. That's what kid brothers are supposed to do. "Hey, Max!" he yelled. "Wait up!"

When they reached the hospital, it was completely consumed in flames. The boys could see smoke and flames pouring from the back of the building.

"Miss Wilson was right," said Max. "It's no use. We're too late."

"Wait! The operating room is in the front," cried Marty. "I had my tonsils out last year, remember? We could look there."

"Let's go!"

They sprinted to the front of the hospital where there was less smoke and hardly any fire. But the blaze was moving quickly in their direction.

"Keep low," ordered Max as they entered the building. "Pull out your shirttail and hold it over your mouth." A wave of hot air hit them when they were inside. They stumbled along a dark corridor, their eyes weeping from the smoke, until they reached some swinging doors.

Marty began to cough. He managed to croak, "This is it. I remember these doors. They lead to the operating room."

They could hear the crackle of flames beyond the doors. Max hesitated. He didn't want to risk his brother's life. He said, "You wait here, Marty. I'll go in alone."

Marty was about to protest. He was very frightened, frightened of the heat and flames beyond the doors, frightened for the safety of his brother. "No, Max, don't go in there. Please don't. Hear that fire? You'll be burned to a crisp."

Just then they heard a moan. Then someone coughed. The sounds came from a small alcove a few feet away.

"Benjie, is that you?" Max shouted. "Benjie! Benjie!"

"Max, it's me. It's me. I'm over here," came a muffled response. The boys heard more coughing.

Max and Marty scrambled through the smoke toward the sounds and found their friend Benjie strapped to a gurney, conscious, but barely. Benjie groaned and held his stomach. "Hurts," he said. "Hurts a lot."

"Quick, Marty! Let's get him outside!" Max said forcefully. They wheeled Benjie's gurney down the corridor and burst through the front doors. By then they were both red in the face, coughing and gasping for breath.

"Keep moving. We've got to get back on the road to Cobalt. Hang on, Benjie." They pushed the gurney down the road for some distance, lifted it over the trolley tracks, and then turned down the path that led to the beach. The Queen Vic was still there, waiting for them.

They unstrapped their friend and helped him aboard. They pushed the boat into the water and while Max made some adjustments to the motor, Marty dipped a cloth into the cool water and placed it against Benjie's forehead.

"That's cool, Marty," said Benjie, smiling weakly. "Thank you. And thank you both for saving me."

"We thought you were a goner, Benjie," Marty said. "The nurses told us you'd been left behind by mistake. And you were dead. What happened?"

"I don't really know, fellas," Benjie mumbled. "I woke up and everybody was gone. And I was strapped down. I figure someone pushed me out of the operating room and into the corridor. Then the gurney must have rolled on its own into that little alcove where you found me. They probably meant to come back for me but never did. Or if they did they failed to see me in the dark and figured someone else had taken me away. I was pretty groggy. Luckily, I was near a small window. It was open a bit and I was able to breathe some air until the time you fellows arrived."

"Now we're going to get you to Cobalt, Benjie. Maybe Dr. Gamble can finish the job and remove your appendix," Max said. "There's a small hospital in Cobalt." He yanked on the starter cord and the motor roared to life.

The town hall in Cobalt was packed to the walls with survivors of the Haileybury fire. Men, women and children sprawled on the pine floorboards. Many chilled survivors who'd been pulled from the lake huddled around a large wood-burning stove.

Others—some with singed arms and shoulders where they'd been struck by flying embers, some who were blinded by the cinders that flew into their eyes, their hair singed and their clothes in tatters, sipped hot tea from cups and mugs. Sandwiches, hot bowls of soup, platters of cakes and cookies were passed around. Blankets and pillows appeared. Soothing ointment and bandages were applied to minor burns and cuts. Some children slept on the hard floor; others amused themselves by playing jacks and hopscotch.

In a corner of the hall, sitting on a stool, an old

man with a lined face thumbed a ball of tobacco into his pipe. When the pipe was lit, he pushed it to the corner of his mouth, turned to the people around him and said, "Strange, ain't it? The flames you flee from on a terrible night like this, the evil embers you curse when they torch your roof and rip through your corn and kill your livestock, are the same friendly coals you count on to heat your soup, toast your bread, warm your house and comfort your body. Fire can warm your hide and bring you joy or it can shatter your life and take all that you own, leaving you stunned and defeated and flat broke." He looked around the hall, and added softly, "The latter is what most of us have experienced tonight."

Amy Mitchell, sick with worry, held one hand to her breast. "Harry, they should have been here long ago. What in the world has happened to them?"

"Honey, there must be a good reason they're not here yet." Harry Mitchell was almost as distraught as his wife was, but he tried not to show it. "It can't be the boat," he said. "It doesn't leak and the motor's in top condition."

Amy rested her head on her husband's shoulder. Her tears began to stain his shirt. "Oh, Harry," she wailed.

Harry patted his wife gently on the back.

Just then the front door flew open and Max and

Marty burst into the room. Their mother flew to them and embraced them. She kissed them repeatedly, even though she knew they both disliked such displays of affection, especially in public.

The boys told their parents about their adventures.

"Then we went back to the hospital and saved Benjie," Marty added. "That was pretty scary."

"We heard that Benjie died in the hospital," Mr. Mitchell said.

"He would have. The staff ran away and left him. But we got him out," Marty said, "It was Max's idea. He was a real hero all night. We just left Benjie with Dr. Gamble."

"Dr. Gamble? Is he here?"

"He and his nurses are here, Dad," Max explained. Doc Gamble and the nurses are over at the hospital. The Doc says Benjie has to have his appendix out."

"His parents are there, too," added Marty. "They thought Benjie had been evacuated from Haileybury with the other patients. Then they were told he was missing and probably dead. His mother fainted when we walked in carrying Benjie."

The hall continued to fill up with refugees from Haileybury and there were cries of excitement and relief when families and friends were reunited. Nobody had any idea how many lives had been lost to the fire. Estimates ranged from only a handful to dozens.

Harry Mitchell pulled out a notepad and a pencil. He went from group to group asking questions, taking notes. Newspaper editors had phoned from several major cities requesting a first-hand account of the tragedy.

"Get in line for some soup, boys," Amy Mitchell said. "When your father's filed his story, we'll go over to Uncle Bill's house and get some sleep."

Max and Marty felt a lot better after they'd eaten hot soup and sandwiches. They canvassed the hall looking for familiar faces. They saw Sally and Agnes across the room and hurried over to visit and catch up. Despite the solemn atmosphere in the hall, the boys were happy to see a number of their friends from school in the crowd.

In the middle of this reunion, someone bawled for silence. "Mayor Pringle wants to say a few words to you all," a man shouted. "So everybody siddown."

Mayor Pringle, small in stature, climbed up onto a soapbox so that he might be seen and heard. He talked about the scope of the disaster as best he could, how the fire had ripped through the community with virtually no warning, how it had swept across the firebreak designed to protect them, how Haileybury was pretty much destroyed. "A few homes to the north of the town may be left standing," he added. "The good news is a cold front is moving in from the north, bringing rain and maybe even snow."

"But too dern late for most of us," one man said bitterly. "That's hardly good news."

Max noticed his father scribbling furiously in his notepad. His father's hand went up.

"Mayor Pringle," he asked, "can you tell us why the firebreak didn't provide us with better protection, as you promised it would?"

"I think I can, Harry," the Mayor sighed. "You see, the men clearing the land to create the firebreak hadn't quite finished the job. The fire swept through the slash and bush that was in that area and moved right into town."

"Just the other day," Mr. Mitchell said, "your wife was quoted as saying you could lawn bowl on that land. What happened?"

A low angry murmur swept through the crowd.

The mayor hesitated. His face turned crimson. He looked to his wife but Mabel was too busy glaring at Amy Mitchell to notice. He decided to tell the truth. If Mabel lit into him later, well, it wouldn't be the first time.

"The work was not done properly," he admitted. Mabel Pringle cleared her throat and looked daggers in his direction. He gulped but continued. "In fact, yesterday I was about to ask the workers responsible for the cleanup—yes, they are related to me by marriage—to make sure they disposed of all the slash and debris they left behind, much of it highly flammable. But before I could speak to them—apparently they were away at their hunt camp for a couple of days—the fire was upon us."

"Do you think the fire moved in from north of town?" Harry Mitchell asked.

"It appears to have, Harry. Yes. From up toward Brooker's Creek."

Max and Marty, sitting on the pine floor, jumped at the mention of Brooker's Creek. Max became flushed in the face and lowered his head to his chest while Marty glanced quickly around the room. He wondered if people were staring at them.

By then, Mayor Pringle was talking about a special relief train that would soon be arriving in town. "Our good friends to the south of us are sending food, blankets, tents, clothing and medical supplies," he told the assembly. "A relief train should be here by noon tomorrow."

A man stood up and said a lot of complimentary things about Haileybury's fire fighters. How they had worked courageously all through the night and saved many lives.

The mayor said, "You bet. They are all heroes and we're grateful to those brave men."

At the back of the hall, a door banged open and two men barged into the room. "I'll show you another real hero," shouted one of the newcomers.

He was a big man with jug ears and dirt on his face.

"That's Wilbur Martin, head of the Haileybury roads department," a man sitting next to the Mitchell boys whispered.

"The poor man he brought with him looks terrible," Max whispered back. "His hair looks awful and his shirt's all burned."

"Listen to me, folks," Wilbur Martin cried out. "This here's my friend Billy Weeks. If you don't recognize Billy it's 'cause his hair was all burned off. And no wonder. Billy drove that old Packard of his back and forth from Charlton to Englehart a dozen times during the night. Then he made half a dozen trips from Haileybury to Cobalt. Carried about a dozen people to safety with every trip. He saved 150 lives tonight. Ain't that somethin', folks? When all of Billy's tires blew out from hitting a culvert he kept right on going, driving on the rims. The fire chased after Billy and burned off the canvas top to his car while flames peeled the paint right off the body. But Billy kept right on going. You're a great man, Billy — you're a hero! And these folks should know it." He grabbed Billy's blackened arm and lifted it in the air.

The room erupted in applause for Billy Weeks. People pounded the shy little man on the shoulders and back. Billy's white teeth showed through a face covered with ashes and soot.

When the applause died down, the mayor cleared

his throat.

"Folks," he said, "there are two more young heroes who deserve our praise and thanks. And they too are in this very room. I've been told that young Max Mitchell and his brother Marty saved several lives during the night. I know the Logan family is extremely grateful to the brothers for alerting them to the fire, that Benjie McNab was rescued from his hospital bed by the boys and that Agnes Witherspoon was rescued from drowning when Max dove into the waters of the lake to save her life."

In the crowd, Agnes Witherspoon smiled. Nobody knew she had only pretended to be drowning. She thought it was a good way to get Max to notice her for a change.

All the people in the hall turned to the Mitchell boys. There was wild applause from all corners. Max and Marty's school friends whooped and hollered their names.

Just then someone shouted from the back of the room. An angry voice boomed out, silencing the applause. "Wait a minute! Wait a dern minute! That's a lot of bunk, Mr. Mayor. Total bunk. The truth is, those Mitchell boys aren't heroes at all. They're anything but. A pair of firebugs is what they are. Arsonists! And they could properly be called murderers, too."

People gasped in shock. Marty nudged his brother. "Max, it's Wilkins, the trolley man."

"I say these two boys deserve a thrashing, not applause," Wilkins shouted. "How can you call them heroes when they're the two who started the fire?" The crowd erupted in confused outbursts of shock and anger and disbelief. "It's true!" Wilkins insisted, his voice rising over the hubbub. He pointed an accusing finger at the boys. "Their sheer stupidity caused the fire that destroyed our town. They should be horsewhipped for their negligence. I say toss them both in jail and throw away the key." Several people shouted out. Some hissed. Wilkins sat down, a sour look of triumph on his face.

Mr. Mitchell jumped to his feet. In his anger he forgot about his role of "objective" reporter.

"Wilkins, you have some nerve accusing my boys of being arsonists," he cried out. "How dare you call them murderers? There's no possible way they could have started the fire. What evidence do you have, mister? Why are you telling such appalling lies?"

Wilkins jumped back up. He ignored Mr. Mitchell and talked directly to the crowd. "I heard it with my own ears, that's how! That girl right there." He pointed at Sally. "She's the one I heard telling her friend all about it. How that Mitchell kid had started a campfire in the woods—up near Brooker's Creek. That he'd failed to put it out! That was just yesterday. That's the fire that burned the town down and killed people."

The room erupted. Everyone began shouting. Sally Logan threw her hands to her face and began to sob. Her father glowered at Max and put one arm around Sally's shoulder.

"That's no proof," Mr. Mitchell shouted. "You can't slander my boys like that. This is outrageous—taking the word of a couple of young girls."

"It's enough proof for me," Wilkins shouted back. "And for most of the people in this room, I'll wager."

"Make 'em pay!" someone bellowed.

"Horsewhip the little firebuggers," cried another.

George Witherspoon motioned for silence. "Max rescued my daughter Agnes from drowning tonight and I'll always be grateful to him for that. Unfortunately, maybe Wilkins is right. One act of heroism might not forgive an act of terrible recklessness. There has to be some form of punishment."

Mabel Pringle, the mayor's wife, sprang to her feet. She wasn't going to miss an opportunity to embarrass Amy Mitchell. "See what happens when parents let a couple of young hoodlums run around loose. There's no discipline today. Young people do what they want when two parents work and the mother's not in the home where she belongs. It's no wonder those boys were off in the woods setting fires." She dealt Max and Marty a withering look. Then she eyeballed her husband, as if to say, "Get up and support me, you little twerp."

Mayor Pringle sighed. He stepped forward and waved his arms until the room fell reasonably silent.

"Folks, before you start thinking about lynching these boys let me have a word with them. See if we can't get to the bottom of this, because some pretty serious charges have been made against them. Max, will you stand up, please?"

Max rose slowly to his feet. His knees were trembling and his face was chalkwhite under the lights.

"Max, were you and Marty fishing at Brooker's Creek yesterday?"

"Yes sir. We were."

"And did you start a campfire while you were there?"

"Yes sir, I did," Max explained. "It was to cook fish on."

"Told you," crowed Wilkins, nodding his head.

"You know how dangerous it is to start a fire in the woods during the forest fire season?" the Mayor asked.

"Yes, sir. That's why I was extra careful. I made a very small fire. It was surrounded by rocks and—"

"Careful, you say. Then I assume you extinguished that fire when you left."

Max hesitated.

"Well, Max. Did you or did you not extinguish that fire?"

Finally he said, "No sir, I can't lie to you. I didn't

put the fire out. It was almost out. But..."

"I knew it," bellowed Wilkins. "I told you so! Didn't I tell you?"

"Why, Max?" the mayor asked.

Max explained.

"Sir, two men came along in a car. They had a gun. They tried to shoot us. That's when we got scared and ran away."

"Bullroar!" shouted Wilkins. "Lies! Why would anyone try to shoot two young kids? That's ridiculous!"

The trolley man's rage was contagious. A wave of hot anger, hostility and indignation swept over the hall. The same folks who'd been applauding the Mitchell boys moments earlier now turned on them.

"Come on, boys," his father said, urging Max and Marty toward the exit. "We need some time to think clearly about all this." Max was relieved. But his father looked stricken, like he had seen a ghost. They steered their way through the jostling throng, like balls in a pinball machine. Max could feel hateful eyes looking at him, condemning him. He heard hateful words thrown at him like a barrage of stones.

"Ignore them," his father whispered as they were pushed, jostled and taunted.

Sally tried to reach Max. Her father held her back. "You're not to have anything to do with him," Mr. Logan said.

Sally turned on her father, "Max saved our lives."

Her father looked away but would not yield.

"Get out of our way," Harry Mitchell threatened, as he pushed through the angry mob. Amy Mitchell was waiting for them at the door.

"What are we going to do, Dad?" Marty asked.

"We're going to your Uncle Bill's house. See if he's home yet from fighting the fire."

Back inside the hall, Sally sobbed uncontrollably. Everything had gone horribly wrong. Max would never speak to her again. Her friend Agnes tried to console her. Then Agnes said something that made matters worse. "Perhaps we've been wrong about Max, Sal. Perhaps he is a thoughtless, selfish person who can turn on the charm like a light switch. If I were you, I wouldn't give him another thought." Agnes turned away, hiding a smile. In her heart, she congratulated herself on a fine performance. Everything had gone exactly as planned.

CHAPTER 11

BACK TO THE SCENE
OF DESTRUCTION

Temperatures plunged overnight. A heavy rain, mixed with snow, moved in from the west, creating clouds of dense smoke over what remained of Haileybury. Most of the fires still blazing were soon extinguished. Alas, the change in the weather came too late to save the town.

In Bill Mitchell's small house in Cobalt, it had been a rough night for everyone. Especially Max. He could think of nothing but the guilt he felt for having started the fire. He had slept fitfully. His parents had not said anything, but Max knew they were worried. His Aunt Elsie had tried to take his mind off the fire. After some hot soup, she had made tea and served slices of lemon meringue pie. "It's Bill's favourite," she had said. "In fact, I don't know anybody who doesn't like my lemon pie."

After the meal they had taken turns scrubbing

themselves clean in the bathtub. Despite his concerns about Max, Harry Mitchell had stayed up most of the night writing a story about the fire. Before dawn, he borrowed Bill's car and drove to the telegraph office where an old friend with nimble fingers relayed his dramatic accounts of the fire to the outside world. His vivid descriptions of the disaster would be seen in newspapers all over North America. His work done, at least for the moment, Harry had returned to his brother's house to pick up his sons.

"Don't wake your mother," he had insisted. "I'm ready to go back to Haileybury. Come on with me. I'll catch some sleep later on."

"Why are we going back, Dad?" Marty had asked groggily. "There's nothing left."

"My friend at the telegraph office told me about a place to stay in Haileybury. We can't stay here. It's not fair to Elsie and Bill. And don't forget, we've got to dig up our strongbox."

On the drive back over the Shore Road, Max and Marty were shocked by the devastation they saw. What had been a forest of towering pines was now like a flat black sea in all directions. The burned husks of several cars smoldered in the ditches.

The rain stopped and Mr. Mitchell turned his windshield wipers off. No one spoke much.

After a while, his father turned and said. "I'm sure

the government will order an investigation into the cause of the fire, Max. You boys will have to answer some questions. Tell the truth and you'll be all right."

"We will, Dad," Marty said.

"I'm not looking forward to that," Max groaned.

Suddenly Marty pointed out the window to the trolley tracks. "Look! There's a bunch of streetcars lined up on the tracks. Must be 20 of them."

"That's right, son," said Mr. Mitchell, turning the car toward the tracks. "And one of them is ours. They've been rushed in from Cobalt and we're going to be living in one of them. At least for a few days. There should be some cots and blankets in them, a small wood stove and even some groceries and bottled water. It may not be like a real home but it's the next best thing."

"Is Mom going to live here too?" Max asked.

"Sure she is. I'm picking her up tonight. It wouldn't be a family without your mom, would it?"

"You've got that right, Dad," chuckled Marty. "What about your work? You've got no office. The newspaper building burned down."

"That trolley car is now my office—and our home," said Mr. Mitchell. "It's the new home of the *Haileyburian*. Uncle Bill has loaned me his old typewriter and a pine table. I'll have my first issue out in a few days. The owner of the paper in New Liskeard will let me use his presses. We may not have many customers or advertisers, but at least we'll have a paper."

"Seems to me it'd be easier just to move away," said Max, "since your son is the bad guy around here."

Mr. Mitchell reached out and put his right hand on the back of Max's neck and squeezed. "You're a good son, Max. Don't forget that."

Their father's spirit and optimism buoyed his sons.

Inside the trolley car, they looked around. "It needs a good cleaning," observed Mr. Mitchell. "Let's get to work, boys."

"Living here is going to be fun," Max said to Marty a few minutes later. Marty was sweeping while Max was polishing the dusty windows. "Imagine living in a trolley car. It's something we'll tell our grandchildren about some day. I'm just sorry we won't be playing any hockey this winter."

"That's been taken care of, too," said Mr. Mitchell. "I ran into the convener of the Haileybury league last night. He says they're already planning to build an outdoor rink on the lake when it freezes over. There's lots of old lumber lying around; some of it scorched but good for rink boards. Snow can be cleared off the ice with wooden scrapers and when the rink needs flooding, they'll chop a hole through the ice and pump up some lake water. It may be windy and cold out there, but you'll have as much fun at hockey as you've ever had. And that's the only reason to play the game anyway—to have fun."

Mr. Mitchell started a fire in the pot-bellied stove.

"Boys, I'm really tired," he said. He lay down on one of the cots. "I was up most of the night. You mind if I get some sleep?"

"Not at all, Dad," said Max. "Say, could we borrow the car for a couple of hours?"

"You want to drive around in this mess? Where do you want to go?"

"Back to Marcella Street. Marty and I could dig up the box we buried in back of the house." Marty noticed his father's eyes were wet.

"The house is gone," he said. His voice sounded far away. "We had some happy times in that house." He tossed Max the car keys. "Be careful." He lay down and was asleep almost before Max and Marty were out the door.

CHAPTER 12

THE MISSING BOXES

Max drove slowly through the town, past the smouldering remains of the Presbyterian Church and past "Millionaire's Row" where the wealthy people lived. "Look! Some of the brick houses survived the fire," he pointed.

"Of course the brick houses survived," said Marty knowingly. "Fire won't touch a brick house. Not if it's red brick."

"Red brick? That's silly," laughed Max. "Now that's a superstition if I ever heard one."

"It's true," insisted Marty. "I read it somewhere. You can see for yourself. All the houses on this street are red brick. Look!"

Max had to admit that Marty was right. All of the surviving homes were red brick. Or a colour close to it. On Marcella Street, Max parked in front of the charred remains of their home. It had burned to the ground. Every familiar thing had gone up in flames and smoke. A few red embers winked at them, as if to say, 'What are you going to do now, Max? You should have put that fire out at Brooker's Creek.'

"We buried the box over here—in Mom's potato patch," he said. "I marked the spot with a stone." He kicked a blackened board aside and found the stone. Then he gasped. Marty, trailing behind, cried out. "What is it, Max?"

"The box is gone!"

Marty slammed the shovel down. "We've been robbed!"

Max looked up and down the street. There was hardly anyone around.

"Marty, let's take a look across the street. See if they took Mrs. Lewis' strongbox. I know she buried one like we did."

They ran across to the remains of the Lewis bungalow. In the soft earth of the flower garden, they saw the edge of a metal box in the blackened soil.

"The crooks didn't come here," Marty said, as they dug up the box. "They probably thought old Mrs. Lewis would have nothing of value." He dusted off the top of the box and turned to his brother. "Think we should open it?" he asked.

"Absolutely not," said Max. "Let's get it across the street and into our car. Mrs. Lewis is going to be a very happy lady when we return it to her."

Max was lugging the box to the Durant when a car

drove slowly down Marcella Street.

"People are starting to return," Max said. "That looks like the Witherspoon's roadster. And there's Agnes. That's weird. She looked right at me, then turned away like she didn't know me."

Marty shrugged. "Women."

They were loading Mrs. Lewis' strongbox into the Durant when they heard the tinkle of a bicycle bell.

"Hey, it's Sally!" Marty said, surprised.

Sally stopped her bike and said, "Hi there, my two heroes."

"Hi, Sally," the boys said, almost in unison. "What are you doing here?"

"I bicycled up from Cobalt to talk with you, Max."

"I can take a hint," Marty said, starting to walk away. "I'll poke around the ruins of our house. See if I can find anything of value. See you later."

It was obvious that Sally was upset. Max could see she had been crying. A small tear spilled from her eye and she quickly wiped it away. "Max, I'm so sorry for what happened. I want you to know that. My big mouth has ruined our friendship and I feel sick about that. I hope you believe me. That's what I came to tell you." Her lower lip trembled as she looked away and wiped away another tear.

"Gosh, Sally, I don't want you to feel bad," Max said awkwardly. He went to her and put his hand on her arm. "It's not your fault. I was wrong to start that fire at Brooker's Creek and I was wrong not to put it out. I know better than that."

"Oh, Max, I know you. You've always been so responsible. Even if you were distracted by something..."

"Thanks, Sal. But it could be my fault. Marty and I are going to drive up to Brooker's Creek later today and check things out. Try to find out for sure if I'm really to blame or not."

"Can I come with you?"

Max hesitated. As much as he would like to have Sally come along, he did not think it was a good idea.

"I don't think so, Sally. But we can drop you off somewhere. We'll even drive you back to Cobalt if you like. We can tie your bike on the roof of the Durant."

"No, no, but you can drive me to our old home-site," Sally replied, managing a smile. "And I'll bicycle back to Cobalt from there after I look around. I want to see if anything survived the fire."

Max called for Marty who came running. Max pulled a large tarpaulin and some ropes from the trunk of the car and threw the tarp over the roof, folding it carefully. He put Sally's bike on top of the canvas. "Help me tie this down, Marty."

"She coming with us?" Marty whispered.

"Just as far as her old house," Max replied. "If

that's okay with you."

Marty's face brightened. "No problem," he said. "Hey, Sally, you sit up front with Max. I'll sit in back with the strongbox."

"What strongbox?" Sally asked, her hand on the car door.

"Old Mrs. Lewis hid her strongbox in her garden. We dug it up for her. Probably not much in it. We'll deliver it to her tonight. Did Max tell you some thief stole our box? Mom and Dad are really going to be upset."

"That's awful. He must have come around at the crack of dawn. Now I'm worried that our old trunk might be gone, too. Maybe it wasn't such a good idea to bury them, after all."

"We'll find out if it's still there soon enough," Max said, "Everybody in? Here we go."

As they drove slowly to the burned out remains of Sally's house, they checked out several backyards and found holes where homeowners had buried metal boxes. At least a dozen were missing. "Those holes are freshly dug," Max observed. "The thieves were busy fellows early this morning. With all the smoke around nobody would have seen them."

"Couldn't one person have done it, Max?" Sally asked.

"No, because of the size of the holes. Some are really large—the size of a trunk. One fellow couldn't carry them himself, but two thieves could clean out Marcella Street in an hour."

"Looks like they went to the homes where they thought there was money—and jewellery maybe," Marty said. "They didn't hit everybody."

"Right," said Max. "Good point, Marty. That means they're local fellows. Men who've lived here long enough to know the town and the people in it."

As they drove on, they found no more holes in backyards.

"I don't think they robbed anyone beyond Marcella Street," Max concluded. "Must have filled a vehicle with the boxes and had no more room."

"Or they ran out of time," Sally suggested. "Some people started coming back to town shortly after daylight. Someone might have seen them if they'd lingered."

They passed the smouldering remains of dozens of houses and barns. They passed the shell of the arena where Max had played so many hockey games. It was the same arena where famous professionals like Cyclone Taylor, Art Ross and Billy Nicholson—the 300-pound goalie—had performed so brilliantly years before when Haileybury, for a season or two, had a team in the National Hockey Association.

"It's all so sad," Sally murmured, dabbing at her eyes with a kerchief.

In the back seat, Marty was preoccupied with the

clasp on Mrs. Lewis' scorched strongbox. He was sorely tempted to open it. And he might have if his big brother's eyes, reflected in the rear view mirror, didn't keep glancing in his direction.

The fire had flattened the Logan house, like all the others for miles around. A brick chimney, like a lonely sentry with nothing to guard, rose from the ashes. Close by the blackened boards that had once been a front porch, hidden in a shallow grave, was the old trunk they'd buried. "Well, that's good news," Sally said, clapping her hands. "My parents have a lot of family heirlooms in there." Max and Marty dug up the trunk and loaded it into the Durant. "We'll deliver it to your folks tonight," Max promised. "Sure we can't drive you back to Cobalt?"

"No, thanks," she said. "Think I'll stay here for a while. I'll think about all the good times we had here."

When Marty climbed up after Sally's bike, she turned to Max.

"What I said before, Max. No hard feelings? We're still friends?"

His heart melting, Max grinned. "Absolutely no hard feelings, Sally," he said. Impulsively, he threw one arm around her shoulder and kissed her on the cheek. Marty grunted as he lifted the bicycle from the roof and pulled the canvas off after it. "Have to do everything myself," he muttered, just loud enough for Max to hear. "Romeo's too busy with more important things." He turned, watched Max and Sally for a second or two, their heads together. Then he shouted, "Hey, that's enough, you two. Come on, Sally, come get your dern bike!"

When they drove away, Max said to Marty, "I don't understand why you don't like Sally. Everybody else thinks she's swell."

"I didn't say I didn't like her," Marty said defensively. "She's all right, I guess. And she's got nice..."

"Nice what?"

Marty turned and gave his brother a devilish grin. Knowing what his brother was thinking, Max burst out laughing.

CHAPTER 13

CHASED BY GUNMEN

The Durant was getting low on gas. Max and Marty were on their way back to Brooker's Creek. Neither boy had much to say. Marty was reading his Hardy Boys book. But he couldn't concentrate.

"I'm so mad I could spit" Marty hissed, thinking about the stolen strongbox.

"It seems like everything makes you want to spit," joked Max. "Keep that up and you won't be able to lick a stamp."

Marty rolled down the car window and spit into the air. The wind rushing by the window caught some of his spittle and threw it back in his face.

"Serves you right!" howled Max.

"Dad is going to be really upset when we tell him someone stole our strongbox," Marty said.

"Maybe we shouldn't tell him just yet," Max had said. "Come on, let's go."

When they arrived at the bumpy path that led

into the woods, Max pulled over to the side of the road and turned the motor off.

"We'll walk in from here," he told Marty. "If I drive in and get stuck or run out of gas I'll really be up the creek."

Marty giggled. "That's a good one, Max. You'll be up the creek all right—Brooker's Creek. What are we doing here, anyway?"

"Come on," said Max, stepping out of the Durant. "Let's check something out. But first I'm going to lock the car. We've still got two strongboxes in the back seat."

They walked briskly down the trail and into what remained of a once-beautiful forest. Blackened stumps stood out from the ground and burnt limbs of trees criss-crossed the area. A red fox scurried away when they approached. "There's at least one survivor," noted Max.

"This place is a disaster area," Marty said. "It's totally burned. The fire destroyed everything. Let's go back. I'm cold and it'll be dark soon."

"Not so fast, Marty. I want to see something for myself."

"What?" asked Marty, struggling to keep up.

"I just want to check the swimming hole at Brooker's Creek. See if our bikes are still there."

"They'll be toast, Max. Burned to a crisp. How could they not be?"

"Marty, I want to make sure, okay?"

Marty sighed. "Okay, big brother. But it's a big waste of time."

They walked on in silence. Then Marty grabbed Max by the sleeve.

"Look, Max, look! Those trees over there are green!"

"Hey, evergreens!" Max exclaimed, walking faster. "And there are some maples and some ash. All untouched by the fire."

"And there's the swimming hole," cried Marty, pointing. "Look, Max! Our bikes are still there, right where we left them."

The Mitchell brothers ran to the spot. "Nothing's been touched by the flames," marvelled Max as he examined the bikes. He noticed some animal tracks in the sand. "Looks like something ate our fish, though."

Marty frowned. "How come the fire missed this place and flattened every place else?"

"It happens sometimes," Max explained. "Sometimes a fire will destroy 1,000 acres and leave a few little acres untouched. A shift in the wind probably spared Brooker's Creek."

"That's great news," Marty said. "Imagine getting our bikes back. I thought they were goners. Let's ride them out of here."

"Don't be so eager, Marty. Aren't you curious

about something else?"

"No, I'm not. I want to get back to the car. What else is there to be curious about?"

"How about the cabin in the woods? And that crazy man who shot at us?"

"Oh, no, Max. Forget about it. We're not going back there?"

"Yes, we are. Those men will be long gone by now. I want to know what they were doing in that cabin—if it's still there. And I wish I knew if they were the fellows who tried to steal our boat."

Through the woods they came to the clearing where the cabin stood, untouched by fire. Nothing stirred. No smoke wafted from the small chimney in the roof. There was no sign of a car. No sounds could be heard from inside the cabin.

Max nudged his brother. "Let's creep closer but be quiet. I'm going to look through the window."

Max slipped along one wall of the cabin until he was standing beside the small window. He took a quick look inside and ducked away, a startled look on his face. Marty, standing well back, knew Max had seen something. Marty shuddered. He fully expected to see a large man carrying a gun bolt from the cabin and begin shooting at him. Marty backed up a step or two and waited for his brother to join him.

"Let's get out of here—fast," Max whispered.

They ran back to Brooker's Creek, retrieved their bicycles and pedalled furiously back down the trail until they reached the place where they'd parked the Durant.

Marty was bursting with curiosity. He tugged on his brother's sleeve. "What did you see in the cabin, Max? What did you see?"

"Marty, I was so surprised I almost fell over," Max said, catching his breath. "There were two men in there. I can't believe they didn't see me. One was asleep on the bed but the other one was cleaning his rifle. Lucky he had his back to me. They were all bundled up in warm clothes and blankets. And there was no fire in the stove."

Marty frowned. "I don't understand. What are they doing there, Max? There was no car, no fresh tire tracks. And why wouldn't they light a fire? I don't get it."

"Neither do I. But it's mighty suspicious. I figure they've hidden their car in the woods. And they may have been afraid to start a fire. Someone might see the smoke and come to investigate." Max snapped his fingers. "Hey, wait a minute! Didn't Dad say something about a bank robbery somewhere north of here? Two guys got away with a lot of cash and disappeared. Dad figured they'd be 100 miles from here by now. Maybe these guys are the bank robbers!"

"Geez," said Marty, his voice rising an octave. "Bank robbers! Let's get Dad. We've got to catch them."

"Not us. That's Sheriff Caldbeck's job, not ours," Max replied. "We'll go find the sheriff. He can come back and decide if they're bank robbers or not."

Marty looked back down the trail and thumbed through his pockets. Max turned to him. "What's the matter? Lose something?"

"Yeah, I had two gloves and now I've only got one. I musta dropped one back there somewhere."

"Well, we can't go back for it now," said Max. "If those guys find it they'll know somebody was poking around outside their cabin. They may come after us. We've got to get back to town right away. Help me get the bikes strapped to the roof of the car. Get some rope and that old tarp in the back seat. We'll tie them down like we did Sally's."

Jesse Jamison looked at his pocket watch. "Getting late," he thought. He yawned and stretched, walked outside and around the corner of the cabin. He stopped beside a tree and began to pee. Autumn leaves fell slowly around him. As he buttoned up, he saw something nestled in the grass and leaves a few feet away. He walked over, bent down and picked up a glove.

"Bert! Come on out here!"

Bert stumbled sleepily from the cabin. "Looks like

a kid's glove."

"It is a kid's glove, you goof. And it wasn't there an hour ago. I'm sure of it. And look! There are footprints under the window. And more footprints over there," He pointed toward the trail. "Somebody's been spying on us. And not more than a few minutes ago."

"A couple of nosey kids, I'll bet." Bert growled. "Maybe they're on their way to the sheriff's office right now. If the sheriff and his boys find us here, Jesse, we're goners. Off to jail again for a good long stretch." Bert shuddered. He hated the thought of returning to a jail cell. "What are we gonna do, Jesse?"

"We're not going back to jail, Bert. We've got to find those kids and take care of them before they can squeal on us. We can't let them yap to the police. Bert, you grab the money and the guns. I'll get the car out of the woods. Maybe those kids walked in here. With a bit of luck we'll catch up to them before they get back to town and open their big mouths about us."

"And if we do catch them, Jesse? What are you planning to...?"

Jesse's arm shot out. His fist caught Bert just below the collarbone. Bert howled in pain.

Jesse's voice was menacing. "You heard me, Bert. Now move! And don't ask questions. Get the guns and the money. You really don't want to know what I plan to do with those kids, so don't ask."

Max had been driving only a minute or two when he saw something in the rear view mirror. A yellow car was approaching them from behind—and it was moving fast! Instinctively, Max hit the gas pedal and the Durant responded with a burst of speed. He said to his brother, "Marty, keep an eye on the car behind us."

Marty spun around and looked out the rear window. "There are two guys in it. They're gonna pass us any second."

But the car behind didn't pull out to pass. It moved right in behind the Durant at full speed. "Go faster, Max!" Marty shouted in alarm. "He's going to plow right into us."

"I'm going as fast as I can!" said Max. He glanced right and left at the deep ditches on both sides of the road.

Buh-bump! Buh-bump! "He's hit us!" shouted Marty.

The Durant shuddered and careened wildly as it was struck from behind—bumper against bumper.

"The fool is trying to kill us!"

"They must be the guys from the cabin in the woods," Max said, wrestling with the wheel. He got the Durant straightened out and tried not to panic.

He changed gears again and the Durant shot ahead. "What are they doing now, Marty?"

"Geez, the guy in the passenger seat has a gun—a rifle. He's leaning out the window. Looks like he's aiming at our tires. Go, Max, go!"

Above the roar of the engine, the boys heard the "Pow!" of a gunshot.

"He missed!" Marty yelled, ducking for cover.

"He'll try again," Max predicted, moving the Durant from side to side across the narrow road. He wasn't going to make the Durant an easy target. If the car lost a tire at this speed, he and Marty would wind up at the bottom of a ditch—and probably be killed.

KA-POW!

The back window of the Durant exploded and bits of glass flew through the air. "He got us that time," Marty screamed. Fortunately, he'd had his head down and was somewhat protected by the two strongboxes in the back seat. "Are you okay, Max?"

"Yeah. Got a nick on my arm, is all. Good thing this is a bumpy road. The potholes are throwing his aim off and he's missed our tires. What's happening now?"

"The guy is reloading but they've fallen back a hundred yards. Their car—looks like a Buick—hit a couple of holes and almost went off the road."

"Marty, open the side window. Reach up and see

if you can loosen the knots holding the bikes in place. Pull the tarp out from under them."

"Hey, I get it. If the bikes fall off, they'll cause the car chasing us to go out of control."

"Yeah, maybe they will. It's worth a try."

In seconds, Marty's nimble fingers had loosened the knots. The rope holding the bikes securely in place fell away and the tarp began to flap in the wind. Marty yanked it off the roof and hauled it into the back seat. Suddenly, both bikes slid off the roof and hit the ground behind the Durant. They bounced crazily along the road, right in the path of the yellow Buick.

CRASH! CRUNCH!

The Buick slammed into the bikes, smashing them to pieces. But the heavy car barely changed course.

"There go our bikes," said Marty, sadly. "I don't know how we can afford new ones."

"That's hardly a priority right now," Max shouted. "Hey, we're almost to Haileybury. They won't shoot at us on Main Street. There'll be a few people around. We'll try to make it to Sheriff Caldbeck's office in one of the trolley cars."

The Durant raced down the almost deserted main street of Haileybury. The car behind them fell back another 100 yards, but it was obvious the men in it weren't going to give up the chase.

"There's the sheriff's office," Max shouted. "But dern it, it's closed."

"Keep on driving, Max," urged Marty. "Let's find Dad."

Seconds later, they skidded to a stop in front of their trolley car.

Max blared his horn several times but nobody appeared.

"Get going!" roared Marty.

Max gunned the engine and the Durant shuddered as he steered it back onto the main road.

"They're almost on top of us," shouted Marty, looking anxiously over his shoulder.

"Maybe Dad is with the sheriff," Max said. "I'll bet they've gone to Cobalt."

"We can't shake them. I'm really scared, Max. Let's get out of here. Step on it."

"Okay! We'll make a dash to Cobalt. Someone there will help us."

"They're right behind us again! And that guy with the gun is halfway out the window. He's aiming it straight at us."

Max weaved the Durant back and forth. He heard two more gunshots.

"Lucky for us this guy is a terrible shot," Max said. "There's Cobalt ahead," shouted Marty.

The Durant sped down the winding main street, its tires squealing on the curves. The Buick was only a few feet behind.

"Marty, I can't stop here in Cobalt," Max yelled. He turned to his ashen-faced brother. "They're liable to jump out and shoot us in cold blood."

"Then keep going Max. Maybe someone will see us and get suspicious. Try honking the horn!"

The two cars roared through town. Max pounded on the horn. People on the wooden sidewalks turned and gawked. The two cars roared through stop signs, splashed through puddles, their wheels sending sheets of muddy water high in the air, soaking people on the boardwalk.

"Those Mitchell kids!" someone shouted as the cars disappeared over a hill.

"As if those crazy boys weren't in enough trouble!"

"Who was that chasing them?" someone asked.

"Don't know. Maybe someone whose house they burned down."

"Someone should tell the sheriff. Have those hoodlums locked up for good!"

Max and Marty were outside the Cobalt town limits headed south at breakneck speed when Max looked at the dashboard and gasped. "We're almost out of gas, Marty. And there's nothing on this road for miles. No houses, nothing. And it's getting dark."

"That Buick is right on our tail, Max. It's a powerful

car. We've got to do something."

"Wait a minute!" Max said, snapping his fingers. "There's an old mining road just ahead on the left. Hang on, Marty. I hope this works."

Just when it appeared the Durant would fly right past the entrance to the mining road, Max yanked on the wheel. The car skewed to the left, throwing pebbles into the bushes and trees, rose up on two wheels and almost tipped on its side. Then it righted itself and shot through the trees that lined the abandoned road.

"What's happening behind us?" Max shouted, leaning forward over the wheel.

"The yellow car flew right past the opening," said Marty. "It must have been doing 100 miles an hour. But I heard the squeal of brakes. So they've stopped to turn around."

"It figures," said Max. "But they haven't caught us yet."

He stepped on the gas, but this time the engine didn't respond. Instead, it coughed once or twice and died. The Durant rolled to a stop.

"We're out of gas," groaned Marty. "Now they'll find us for sure."

Max grabbed Marty by the hand and pulled him across the seat and out of the car. "Come on, let's run for it. I've got an idea." He reached in the back seat and grabbed the tarp.

The boys raced down the mining road.

"What's your big idea?" asked Marty, breathing hard.

"I know this area," Max replied. "Up ahead there are some old mines and deep holes dug in the ground. I used to bicycle in here with some of the guys a couple of years ago. Until Dad said it was too dangerous. One of the fellows fell down a hole one day and we couldn't get him out. It was about ten feet deep—and wide. The fire department had to come and rescue him with a ladder."

"We better be careful then 'cause it's getting dark. And we must be getting close to the lake. Hey, Max, we could jump in the lake. We're probably better swimmers than those goons behind us."

Max said, "No, we can't do that. There's a steep cliff that runs down to the lake. And rocks below. We can't escape that way."

"Then we're trapped in here," Marty said glumly. "Is that what you're saying?"

Max didn't want to admit it, but his brother was right. They were trapped. After a few more strides, Max said, "Whoa! Let me go ahead." He moved forward tentatively, looking for a deep hole in the ground.

"There it is," he said, pointing ahead. "It's more of a pit than a hole."

Max gave an order. "Get me some branches off those evergreens, Marty."

While his brother obediently snapped branches off the nearest tree, Max unfolded the brown tarpaulin he'd been clutching under his arm and threw it over the pit. He found half a dozen rocks and placed them on the edges of the tarp. Acting quickly and quietly, he took the branches from Marty and laid them carefully on top of the tarp and the rocks. "It's not the greatest camouflage but it may do," he grunted. "Especially in the dark."

"Hey, neat," said Marty, admiring his brother's handiwork. "It's a trap—just like I saw in a jungle movie once. The hero trapped a leopard that way. Or was it a polar bear?"

"If it was the jungle and it was a polar bear, he was a long way from home," snapped Max.

He grabbed Marty by the wrist and guided him around the pit until they stood in the path on the other side.

"Listen, I hear them coming," whispered Marty.

"They're driving slowly because it's so dark and the road's all overgrown," said Max. "When they find our car they'll stop and search it. They'll figure we'll be hiding in the back seat. Or under the car."

"So? Then what?" asked Marty.

"Then we've got to lure them in this direction. We don't want them getting back in their car."

Just as Max predicted, the men pursuing them stopped when they came upon the Durant.

Max and Marty could hear the sound of car doors slamming and muffled voices 100 yards away.

"I think one of them has a flashlight," whispered Marty. "He's using it to look inside and under the Durant."

"You're right," said Max. "Now I want you to kneel down and clutch your knee. Pretend you've wrenched it and you can't walk."

"Which knee, Max?"

"Geez, Marty, it doesn't matter. Just do it." He pushed Marty to the ground. Then he cupped his hands and shouted, "Help! Help! We need help here."

Through the darkness he could see a beam of light turn toward him. He could vaguely see two figures moving quickly in his direction. "Help!" he shouted. "My brother fell and broke his leg. He needs a doctor."

The two men rushed closer. The beam of their flashlight caught Max in the eyes. Then the beam flashed to Marty who gripped his knee and let out a howl of pain.

"You boys stay right where you are," a gruff voice said. "We'll take good care of you. My friend here's a doctor."

Max sprang into action. "Marty! Get up! Run for it!"

The brothers sprinted down the path. The men started after them. But they didn't get far. Max and Marty heard their screams and curses when they stepped on the tarp and it gave way beneath their feet. They tumbled into the deep hole.

Max and Marty stopped running.

"It worked!" Marty shouted. "Max, you're a genius!"

At the lip of the hole, the boys looked down. Foul language drifted up from the bottom of the pit. One of the men lay on his back, cradling his leg. "I've done broke my ankle," he groaned.

"Serves you right, you blockhead," his partner snapped. "If you could shoot straight, we wouldn't be in this mess."

The glow of the flashlight lit his face. Max and Marty gasped. It was Mr. Jamison!

Marty stepped on something hard and looked down. It was the rifle! "Guess you won't be needing this anymore," he taunted the men.

Max took Marty's arm. "Come on," he said, "These two dumbbells aren't going anywhere."

"Who you calling a dumbbell?" shouted the injured man.

Jamison sneered. "You! You jackass."

The two boys burst out laughing.

On the way up the road, Marty stopped.

"But our car is out of gas," he said.

Max laughed. "I know. But theirs isn't. Maybe they left the keys in it."

Gently, he took the rifle from his brother. "Better let me carry this."

CHAPTER 14

ARRESTED

Sheriff Caldbeck was excited. He was leading a convoy of cars racing south from Cobalt. He was about to arrest two dangerous criminals. He hadn't made a major arrest in years. This was his big chance. Bank robbers! If what those two Mitchell kids said was true, he'd become a hero in the community. By tomorrow, folks would have a lot more to talk about than the big fire. They'd be talking about him, the man who made the Big Arrest.

Earlier that evening, he'd driven to the Cobalt town hall with Harry Mitchell. He'd been asked to speak to the survivors of the fire about policing the community. Harry and Amy Mitchell were worried about their sons, who'd borrowed the Durant earlier in the day and hadn't returned.

"We'll go looking for them right after my little talk," the sheriff had promised. "They probably ran out of gas somewhere."

His words were barely spoken when the doors to the hall flew open. Max and Marty ran in, breathing hard.

"Sheriff! Dad! Come quick!" Max cried. "We've trapped the fellows who robbed the bank. They're stuck in a big hole."

"They were going to shoot us dead," Marty added.

"Someone tried to shoot you?" their father said, reaching for his coat. "Where are they? And where's the Durant?"

"They're trapped in a pit down the old mining road. We'll need a ladder to get them out. The Durant is there too, but it's out of gas. We'll need to bring some. Hurry! Let's go!"

Marty helped his father into his coat. Marty was bursting to tell what had happened. "We were really scared, Dad, but Max outsmarted those two creeps. We had to jog back to Cobalt. We were going to drive the robber's car back, but one of them had the keys. Max looked down the hole and asked to borrow them. I can't repeat what they told him to do."

Sheriff Caldbeck slowed down and turned on to the mining road. Other cars followed and quickly fanned out around the large hole in the ground, the beams from headlights crisscrossing like searchlights.

The Mitchell brothers ran to the yellow Buick.

"There's a bag in the back seat with money spilling out of it," Max called out.

"And there's a gun in the front seat!" Marty shouted.

"Don't touch anything!" Sheriff Caldbeck shouted back. "That's our evidence. Say, how come the tires are flat?"

"I thought of that," Marty said proudly. "I told Max the robbers might get out of the hole somehow. So we let the air out of their tires."

"Smart thinking, son," said the sheriff, patting Marty on the back. By the way, I brought an extra can of gas for the Durant. Say, have you got your camera with you?"

"It's in the car, sir. Covered with broken glass from the shattered window." He looked at his father and shrugged. "Sorry, Dad."

"Better get it," the sheriff said in a whisper. "You can get some shots of me making a big arrest." He patted his right cheek. "This is my best side."

The Cobalt town hall was filled to capacity that evening. People were there to discuss plans to rebuild Haileybury. Mayor Pringle called the meeting to order but he had difficulty getting their full attention. Everyone was buzzing about the Big Arrest.

Suddenly there was a commotion outside the hall. The door flew open and Sheriff Caldbeck rushed in. "We've got 'em!" he shouted. "Found the bank robbers right where the Mitchell boys said they were. You can see them for yourselves." He motioned to his deputies. The prisoners, their heads down and hands cuffed in front of them, were escorted in. Harry Mitchell and his sons filed in behind them.

"Let me have your attention, folks," bellowed the sheriff.

"I want Max and Marty Mitchell to come forward. I'm recommending they receive the 1,000-dollar reward that the bank has offered for the arrest of these crooks. The boys earned it."

One of the people in the crowd, the trolley man Wilkins, had heard enough. "Sheriff, I can't believe you're going to give a reward to two kids who burned down the town!" he shouted angrily. "That's ridiculous. You should punish them, not reward them. Besides, I've been told those two aren't just arsonists. No sir! They're thieves too. They were seen digging up strongboxes all over town!"

The audience in the hall erupted in shouts.

"Now, just a minute." The sheriff waved his hands in the air for silence. "There's something you folks should know—something important. But I think Max Mitchell should come up and tell you himself. Max, come on up here." Reluctantly, Max stepped forward, clearing his throat. Nervously, he spoke to the crowd. "Marty and I borrowed my dad's car and drove up to Brooker's Creek today. We were hoping to find proof that we weren't responsible for the fire that destroyed Haileybury. And I believe we did. If you go up there, you'll find that nothing at all was burned at Brooker's Creek. No trees, no grass, nothing. Our bikes were right where we left them—in perfect shape."

"But not anymore," Marty shouted, pointing at the prisoners. "Those two goofballs ran right over them. That was after we found them hiding out in an old cabin. Then they chased us and tried to kill us."

The sheriff looked over at Jesse and Bert. "Is that right, Jamison? You two birds were laying low in that cabin? It didn't burn down?"

"The Mitchell kid is right, sheriff," Jesse said. "The big fire spared that place and a few others north of here. We thought we'd stay in the cabin until things cooled off a bit. And we didn't try to kill the Mitchell kids. They were spying on us so we thought we'd throw a bit of a scare into them."

"You shot at them didn't you?" the sheriff snorted. "I'm going to charge you two with attempted murder. That and the bank robbery. Then there's the matter of the strongboxes which you've no doubt hidden somewhere."

Jesse Jamison was outraged. "Now hold on, sheriff. We may be bank robbers. But we're no petty thieves."

"See!" thundered Wilkins. "They didn't steal the

boxes. I know someone who saw the Mitchell kids take them. Eyewitnesses! This witness saw you boys digging one up and putting it in your car this morning. Caught you red-handed in Mrs. Lewis' backyard. I just ran out to look in your car and, what do you know? There's a strongbox and a trunk in the back seat. Still covered in dirt. How do you explain that?"

"Well, Max," said the sheriff. "What about it?"

Everyone began to holler and shout. Then Sally Logan pushed her way through the crowd.

"I was on Marcella Street this morning," said Sally, glaring at Wilkins. "I saw Max and Marty put the Lewis strongbox in their car. They told me they were going to return it to Mrs. Lewis tonight. Then they drove me back to my house—well, it's not a house anymore—but to where I used to live. On the way, we passed places where strongboxes and trunks had been removed from the ground. I know Max and Marty didn't take them. They couldn't have."

Wilkins sneered. "Maybe you helped them steal those boxes, dearie. You're pretty close with Max, aren't you? And there's a lot of money and jewels missing. Pretty girls like you love jewellery."

Sally was appalled. She cried out, "Mister, how dare you insinuate I'm lying. How dare you call me a thief. Maybe YOU stole the boxes!"

"You tell 'em!" someone shouted.

"Maybe Wilkins is right," countered another.

Sally gave Max an agonized look, turned and started to run out of the room.

When she reached the cloakroom by the front door, Agnes Witherspoon grabbed Sally by the arm.

"How does it feel to know your boyfriend is nothing but a liar and a thief?" Sally wrenched free of Agnes. Without thinking, she struck Agnes across the cheek with her open hand. The blow stunned Agnes. Her mouth flew open and she staggered back, falling into the arms of her parents. "Booo, hooo," she wailed.

Sally leaned close to her ear and hissed, "You're such a little troublemaker, Agnes. I know now it was you who started badmouthing Max. It was you who spread the word about him starting a fire. And you who said he was stealing strongboxes. You were my friend once and I trusted you. I never knew how jealous you were. Now I think you're...you're...contemptible." With a toss of her curls and her head held high, Sally walked out the door.

"Atta girl, Sally," Marty shouted. "Max, I'm really beginning to like that girl."

"She's something, isn't she?"

"She sure is. And she's got great..."

"Never mind that," Max said sharply.

CHAPTER 15
ANOTHER MYSTERY TO SOLVE

The Mitchells slept in their new home that night. The pot-bellied stove threw plenty of heat. Mrs. Mitchell had even found time to hang some curtains over the windows.

Though relieved to learn of their sons' innocence, the parents were annoyed neither boy had mentioned anything about being shot at during their trip to Brooker's Creek.

"It's my fault," Max said. "But I wasn't quite sure the first gunshots were aimed at us. And when I asked Jesse Jamison about it tonight, he assured me he was shooting at a rabbit."

"There's no excuse for their actions," Amy added. "I have no sympathy for them, especially the one named Bert." She shuddered to think of how cruel he'd been.

The next morning, the boys found their father hard at work writing follow-up stories about the great fire.

"Then I have to write about the bank robbers and how my two sons helped catch the holdup men. I'm going to be here most of the day."

"Would you mind if we borrow the car again, Dad?" Max asked.

"I suppose it's all right," he said. He tossed Max the keys. "Just promise me you'll try to bring it back without any more bullet holes in it." He winked. "There's another meeting of the Haileybury citizens in Cobalt this afternoon but the sheriff can drive your mother and me there in his car. How about we meet you there?"

In the car, Marty asked, "Where are we off to now?"

"Back to Cobalt."

"Why?"

"A hunch," said Max. To Marty's frustration, he wouldn't say another word.

Max pulled up to the curb in front of a Cobalt poolroom.

Marty looked skeptical. "We playing pool?"

Max laughed. "Not you, little brother. Sit still. I'll be back in a minute."

The poolroom was filled with smoke. Players were bent over tables and Max heard the sharp "clicks" of balls cracking against each other on the green cloth—and the "thunk" of balls disappearing down small holes. He stared through the smoke haze. At a table near the back of the room stood Elmer and Barney Dooley. They were playing in a match against two Cobalt men. The competition appeared to be intense.

Max slipped into a chair along the wall. Next to him, a pale-faced teenager was watching the shots intently.

"Hi," Max said, "How's it going? Looks like this is a pretty serious match?"

"Sure is," he answered. "It's always serious when Haileybury guys play Cobalt guys. A lot of money goes to the winners."

They watched in silence as the match continued. It was obvious that all four players had spent a lot of time in poolrooms. Finally, one of the Cobalt men sank the remaining black ball and the game was over. The Cobalt boys smirked and patted each other on the back. Elmer and Barney matter-of-factly reached for their wallets.

"Watch this."

Max saw Elmer and Barney casually count out ten bills each, then flick them on to the table. The Cobalt boys scooped up the bills like hawks after a family of field mice.

"Wow!" said Max. "That's a lot of money."

"That's nothing. Those two Haileybury fellows have dropped about 500 dollars since they came in a couple of hours ago," his companion said.

"Let's take a break," Elmer told Barney. We'll head down to the tavern."

At the door, they passed in front of Max.

"Excuse me, fellows, you got a minute?"

Barney said, "Hey, I know you. You're the kid who burned down Haileybury."

"What do you want, bud?" Elmer said bluntly.

Max flashed what he hoped was a winning smile. "I'm doing some work for my dad. You know, the owner of the *Haileyburian*."

"Yeah, we know him. Harry Mitchell. Puts out a lousy paper."

Especially if you haven't learned to read, Max was tempted to retort, but he decided to hold back the insult.

"I'm writing a story on the bear population in this area. I was told that you fellows know a lot about bears and their habitat."

"What habits?" asked Elmer.

"No, their habitat. You know, where they live, their territory—that sort of thing."

Barney laughed. "Kid, somebody's been pulling your leg. We don't know nothing about bears, except they're brown and fat and ugly. And if you run into a female with cubs, you don't try to feed her out of your hand."

"And they've got bad breath," added Elmer.

"But somebody told me you fellows were talking

about a cave or a den you discovered around here. I thought you could show me where it is. I'd like to take a photo of it for the paper."

Elmer shot Barney a startled look. He said coldly, "You're mistaken, kid. That wasn't us."

"It wasn't?"

"We don't know nothin' about a bear's cave. Musta been somebody else."

Max said, "Okay, then. Sorry to bother you. And I'm sorry you lost so much money at pool. Since we're all from Haileybury, I was rooting for you to win."

"Don't worry about it, bud," Elmer said, winking at his brother. "There's plenty more money where that came from."

The men laughed and headed for the door. They jumped into a green Ford and took off.

"Where did they get that car?" Max wondered.

In the Durant, Marty put down his Hardy Boys book and sighed. "Well, what was that all about?"

Max grinned. "Never mind. I'll tell you later. Now we're going back to Haileybury."

When Max reached Haileybury he turned the Durant off the Shore Road and headed west of the town, driving out the Old West Road.

"Marty, do you know the old Johnston farm?" he asked.

"Sure. It's got a big red barn on the property."

"Well, it's around here somewhere. Or it used to be. See the remains of that mailbox in the ditch up ahead. See if you can read the name on it."

Max came to a stop and Marty leaned out the window. "I can read part of it. It says JOHN something.... The rest is all scorched."

"Then this must be it. Look! Everything's gone but part of the red barn. There's one wall still standing. We'll drive down the Johnston's lane and park the Durant behind it. Just in case someone comes nosing around. We'll walk in from there."

"Be careful," Marty cautioned. "There are deep ditches on either side of their drive. Filled with water and muck."

Max parked the car out of sight. Then he and Marty walked across a blackened field until they came to a fenceline. Beyond the twisted wire there were several small hills.

"I sure wish you'd tell me what you're up to," Marty griped. "Don't treat me like a kid. What's the big secret?"

Max ignored the question. He said, "Look for an opening in one of these hills. Look for a small cave. A cave full of bears."

"Yikes!" Marty exclaimed, stopping. "Bears! Let's get out of here."

Max laughed. "I'm just kidding. I'm looking for an abandoned bear cave."

On the side of the next hill, they found it, a gaping hole big enough for them to walk into without even bending over.

"It would have been hard to find this opening before the fire," Max observed. "The undergrowth would have covered it. Elmer and Barney must have found it when they were clearing the land around here. Let's slip inside."

"Wait a minute," Marty said. "What do Elmer and Barney have to do with this? I don't get it." But Max had already disappeared into the cave. Marty turned and spit into the wind before hurrying after him.

The boys shuffled forward, waiting for their eyes to adjust to the darkness of the cave. It was much bigger than they anticipated and seemed to go back a good distance.

Marty giggled. "If there are some bears asleep in here, I may never speak to you again," he said nervously. "Hey, what's that over there?"

Deep in the cave, something lumpy caught their attention. Max moved closer. "It's a tarpaulin," he said. "And it's covering something. Now this is interesting."

He lifted the tarpaulin and pulled it back.

Marty gasped. "Geez, Max, it's a bunch of strongboxes."

"Right, Marty. Metal boxes. And some wooden ones. Big ones and small ones. And I'll bet they all came from Marcella Street. In fact, there's Dad's strongbox over there. I know he put some money in it. See if it's still there."

Marty opened the familiar box. "Nope," he said, "No money. Just the other stuff Dad put in it. And some of Mom's stuff is here. All the cash is gone."

"Looks like my hunch paid off."

"What is going on, Max?"

"Listen, when Jesse said he and Bert didn't know anything about missing strongboxes, I believed them. So who could have done it? I thought of Elmer and Barney. But there was no evidence that they stole them, no real proof."

"Well, this looks like proof to me," Marty said, nodding toward the boxes.

"Sure it is. I saw the Dooleys betting wads of money at the poolroom. And they just bought a car. Where do you think they got that much cash? Right out of these boxes. And a lot of it from our box because Dad had some money he meant to put in the bank but didn't have time. I figured the boxes might be here when I asked the Dooleys if they knew anything about a bear cave. They looked surprised and denied it. But the other day, we distinctly heard them talking about such a cave to the men on the street. So I knew they were lying to me."

"And that's when you knew..."

"Yep. I knew they must be the thieves who dug up

the boxes. And where better to hide them than right here where they'd been clearing the slash? They're probably kicking themselves for mentioning the cave at all, but at that time they didn't know they'd be needing it for a hiding place."

"They both have tongues that flap like a flag," Marty said. "So what'll we do now? I want to get out of this cave. It's cold in here."

"Quiet," Max said in a whisper. "Somebody's coming. Let's move back in the cave. It's pitch dark back there."

They crept deeper, following the contours of the cave. The passageway turned sharply to the right. Just ahead Max thought he saw a glimmer of light. "Wait here," he said.

He was back in a few seconds. "There's a small hole, an exit hole," he whispered. "We may be able to squeeze through it and come out on the other side of the hill."

"Let's go," Marty whispered back, his voice trembling. "I'm going to wet my pants if I stay here another minute."

"No, you're not. Stay calm. We're better off to wait it out. They may not stay long. They probably came for more cash."

The boys could hear Elmer and Barney talking.

"Let's get some more money and get out of here," Elmer said. "People are moving back to town and

163

someone might see us and get suspicious. From now on we should come here only at night."

"Ah, you worry too much," Barney complained. He frowned. "Hey, did you remove the tarp covering the boxes?"

"I never touched it. You put it there."

"Well, it's not covering them now. And my fairy godmother sure as heck didn't do it. Light a match, will you."

The boys heard the "scrrrit, scrrrit," of a match flaring to life.

"Geez," said Elmer, "Lookit them footprints around the boxes. Somebody's been in here messin' around. Take a look around."

"Come on," Max whispered. "We're in big trouble. Let's try to get out of here."

Footsteps approached. Barney Dooley was coming toward them—fast.

Max took Marty by the arm and motioned him to be quiet. Then Max turned and growled deep in his throat.

"Grrrr—awww!"

Barney turned and bolted toward the front of the cave.

"What the..." said a startled Elmer as Barney bowled over his brother like a linebacker nailing a quarterback. They sprawled in the dust.

"There's a bear back there!" whimpered Barney.

"Must be ten feet tall. He was ready to chew my leg off, Elmer. I saw his shadow. He's huge, I tell you."

Elmer sprang to his feet and shoved his brother. "That's bull, you wimp. How do you know it's a bear?"

"I heard him snarl. He was ready to chew my leg off. And I saw his shadow. He's huge, I tell you."

Elmer shoved his brother. "What a scaredy cat you are!" he sneered. "Yellow as a school bus. Those weren't bear prints we saw around the strongboxes. They were footprints. Let's go see who made them."

Meanwhile, Max and Marty had hurried through the darkness and stood beneath the hole. It was just above their heads. Max leaped up and managed to get his head and shoulders through the opening. He braced himself with both hands and shot up out of the hole. He kicked a couple of small rocks, which clattered noisily. He reached back into the hole and grabbed Marty's outstretched hands in his.

"Hurry, Max, hurry. They're coming fast."

Gritting his teeth, Max yanked his brother up through the opening and out of the cave. The boys leaped to their feet and ran swiftly over and around the small hills toward the burned out red barn and their Durant.

By the time they ran behind the barn and jumped into the car, breathing hard, they could hear shouts behind them. Elmer and Barney were lumbering along after them. They were furious. The big-bellied Dooleys were no match for the Mitchell boys when it came to speed afoot. But they were smart enough to turn and take a shortcut, hoping to get ahead of the boys and cut them off.

Behind the wheel, Max started the car and spun the Durant around, pointing it down the lane of the Johnston property. But turning the vehicle and getting it out from behind the barn had taken several seconds. Max looked up. Barney Dooley was planted directly in his path, pointing his finger as if to say, "I've got you now." Then Elmer Dooley emerged from a ditch, carrying a broken fence post that he was swinging like a baseball bat.

"Their Ford is blocking the road!" shouted Marty.

"I know!" shouted Max.

Barney picked up a large rock and the two men advanced toward Max and Marty.

"Hold on, Marty!" Max gunned the engine.

"No way the kid's gonna run us down," Elmer smirked. "No guts."

His brother grinned wickedly and swung the broken post in an arc, like a batter warming up. "Hold steady!" he bellowed.

The Durant roared forward. At the last second, the Dooleys dived sideways into a mucky ditch. The Durant whizzed past them but near the end of the lane, Max slammed on the brakes. The car threw up a cloud of dust.

"Listen, Marty," said Max. "Jump out and take the Ford out of gear. Put it in neutral." Marty sprang from the Durant and was back in seconds. "Okay," he said.

Max edged the Durant forward until the bumpers of the two cars clicked. Marty looked over his shoulder and saw the Dooleys, scrambling out of the ditch. "Hurry, Max! Those guys want to murder us."

Max accelerated. The Ford edged backwards.

"Faster!" screamed Marty. Max dropped his foot hard on the pedal. He grinned when he saw the Ford's steering wheel start to waggle. The Ford rolled into the muddy ditch and tipped over on its side. Max stepped on the gas and turned onto the Old West Road.

He heard Marty shout. "Look out!"

Elmer Dooley, running hard, had leaped on the running board. His thick arm shot through the open window. His muddy hand grabbed Max by the throat.

"Marty!" Max croaked. "Help me!"

Marty reached into the back seat and grabbed the shovel they had used the day before. He leaned across Max and whacked Elmer Dooley's arm and shoulder with the blade of the shovel, using a short choppy blow. Elmer howled in pain. He released his grip on Max, tumbled off the running board and hit the ground with a "thunk." His big body somersaulted backward into the ditch.

"Tarnation!" he thundered when he found himself submerged in a pool of stagnant water. When he rose to his knees a lily pad was stuck in his hair and a green frog clung to his nose.

"Where's the other one? Where's Barney?" Max shouted.

"Don't worry about Barney," chuckled Marty. "He's back there, completely winded. He threw a rock at us and made a dent in Dad's car. Dad's not going to like that."

"We can't worry about that now," said Max. "They won't get their car out of that ditch, not without a tow. By the time the Dooleys walk back into town we'll have a reception committee waiting for them."

CHAPTER 16
MORE CULPRITS CAPTURED

Max and Marty found Sheriff Caldbeck talking to their parents in front of their trolley car home. The sheriff's car was idling nearby.

"We were just leaving for the meeting in Cobalt," said Mr. Mitchell. "You boys coming?"

"Dad, we can't. And neither can the sheriff," Max said. "We need him to come with us."

"What now?" asked Mr. Mitchell.

"Later, Dad. C'mon, sheriff," said Max. "Oh, Dad? You and Mom better come too. We'll explain everything on the way."

They spotted the two Dooleys trudging along the main road to town.

"They look like wet scarecrows," said Amy Mitchell. "I wonder what Mabel Pringle will think of her dear little brothers after this."

Sheriff Caldbeck stopped his vehicle. He shook his head. "What a pair of losers." He handcuffed the pair, and then stood back.

"Whew, you boys stink. And I'm darn sure I don't want you in my squad car all covered with mud and the like. Would you mind walking the rest of the way into town?"

Barney Dooley nodded sadly. "Why not?" he grumped. "We ain't had a very good day."

"Marty," the sheriff asked, "you got your camera? A photo of this arrest might be good for the front page of the *Haileyburian*."

"It's in the car, sheriff. I'll get it. By the way, sheriff, which is your good side again?"

The meeting in Cobalt was well underway when the Mitchells arrived. Despite the tragedy of the fire, the mood was less gloomy. It was upbeat and optimistic. People stood up and announced they were anxious to return to Haileybury, and eager to tackle the job of rebuilding their town.

"It was the best dern town I ever lived in," said one oldtimer, "and it will be again."

"If we start to rebuild tomorrow," Mayor Pringle said, "we can have a lot of houses up—or partway up—before the real cold weather comes. Meanwhile, there are lots of tents available. And we can get more trolley cars to live in."

Principal J.H. McFarlane said he planned to stay on, even if it meant teaching in a tent. "We have many talented, dedicated students in Haileybury and

I want their education to continue. And so does all of my staff."

"That's wonderful news," said the Mayor. The crowd applauded.

A railway man stood up. "There's a train headed here from the south full of clothing, lumber and supplies. All donated by people in the big city. And they tell me there's more to come."

"And I hear the government is willing to help out financially," another man said. "With loans and grants."

There was more applause, louder this time.

"We'll do it," shouted Mayor Pringle. "That's the spirit, folks. We'll build a new Haileybury and make it a jewel on Lake Temiskaming."

He paused for a moment. Then he added a serious and personal comment.

"As your mayor, folks, I've always tried to level with you. The truth is, Mrs. Pringle left on the train for Toronto today and there's not much chance she'll be coming back."

The crowd uttered a sympathetic, "Ohhh."

"It's going to be all right," the mayor smiled. "We'll get through this. After all, we're Haileyburians." That raised the loudest applause of all.

Sheriff Caldbeck stood up and hollered for attention. "Beg pardon, Mayor. I wonder if I might make an announcement."

The crowd hushed. The Sheriff told them the story about the Dooleys and how they had robbed people in town of their strongboxes. He surprised them by saying, "It didn't help none that these two lazy fools and their shabby work led to the fire that destroyed our town."

The crowd booed and hissed. The Mayor hung his head when the Dooleys were mentioned, ashamed of his relationship to them. He decided to make a motion. "Based on what's happened, I think it might be a good idea for me to resign," he sighed.

The crowd shouted, "No!" and "You're our Mayor!" and "Don't quit, Percy!"

The Mayor was deeply touched and quietly nodded his thanks.

"A couple more things," said Sheriff Caldbeck. "It was the Mitchell boys who uncovered the truth about the Dooleys. Not me. They found the cave where the strongboxes were hidden. If it wasn't for the Mitchells, we might never have known the Dooleys set fire to the field they were clearing. Careless smoking did it. While they were taking a nap, high winds came along; the grass fire the Dooleys caused merged with the forest fire and that meant the town was doomed. The Dooleys even stole the Mitchells motor boat when they panicked and ran away."

The Sheriff spotted a familiar face in the crowd. He couldn't resist saying, "Cat got your tongue, Mr.

Wilkins? No more accusations to make against the Mitchell boys? Still think I should lock them up and throw away the key? Well, Mr. Wilkins?"

Wilkins squirmed in his chair, turned red in the face and stared down at the floor.

Mayor Pringle took over.

"Folks, it's time we gave credit where credit is due. And we haven't given nearly enough credit to those intrepid young men, Max and Marty Mitchell. Many of the accusations against them were made in haste and all are regrettable. On your behalf, I apologize to them and I think they've earned an oldfashioned North Country ovation."

Max and Marty were frozen in surprise. They were hoisted on to the shoulders of two burly lumberjacks and paraded around the room. People cheered and applauded and shouted, "Well done, Mitchells."

Max saw a special someone at the back of the hall and she was applauding. She blew him a kiss. Marty raised both hands over his head like he'd seen the heavyweight boxing champion do in the newsreel at the Bijou. He noticed his mom dabbing at her eyes with a lace hankie and suddenly, tears began falling down his cheeks. His throat was so dry he couldn't have spit if there was a bet on it. Someone started singing "For He's a Jolly Good Fellow" and everyone joined in. And that was followed by one last ear-splitting roar. It was a moment the boys would remember for the rest of their lives.

Then they were down, off the shoulders and back on their feet, light-headed but laughing.

The bedlam subsided and Max made his way through the crowd to Sally.

"Hello, hero," she smiled.

Max blushed. "Hush," he said. "It will always be just Max to you."

She took him by the arm. "Okay, Just Max. I've got the family car. Can I offer you a drive home?"

Home, Max thought. The word never sounded better than it did at that moment.

THE REST OF THE STORY

It's a miracle that more people didn't perish in the great fire in the North Country. Statistics gathered by officials in the area revealed that 43 people died, over 1,500 families were burned out and over 6,000 people were left homeless. The total property loss was over six million dollars. One prominent politician showed genuine concern for the fire victims and journeyed to Cobalt on the day following the disaster to survey the devastation and to assure the victims of financial help. He personally donated 500 dollars from his own pocket, stating, "I would like to contribute more but, as everybody knows, I am not a wealthy man." Within a month of his appeal for material aid, over 150 railroad cars filled with clothing and other necessities arrived in the community. Women who sorted through piles of clothing even found evening gowns and swimsuits which, of course, they tossed aside in favour of woolen sweaters, heavy coats and winter boots.

A major city far to the south found a large number of old streetcars stored in barns and sent them north. Survivors of the fire were overjoyed when the ancient cars arrived. Occupants filled seams in the wooden sides of the cars with paper and cloth, installed wood-burning stoves and used them as temporary homes throughout the winter months.

The Red Cross set up a hospital in Haileybury and people were ordered to boil their drinking water when typhoid germs were found in the lake. A telegraph office was established in an old boxcar.

Tents with stovepipes poking through their canvas tops and all kinds of makeshift shacks sprang up on the hillside overlooking the lake while construction workers toiled long hours rebuilding the business district as well as individual homes.

Two banks were soon in service, one located in a house, the other in a garage.

J. H. McFarlane, the public school principal and the town's eminent scholar (my grandfather) retained his excellent corps of teachers and classes were held in a portable building. One of his four sons, Leslie McFarlane, went on to a distinguished writing career, including authorship of the first 21 books in the immensely popular Hardy Boys books under the pen name, Franklin W. Dixon. For his efforts he received the sum of 100 dollars per book and no royalties. The books sold in the millions.

Leslie McFarlane was my father and I have always considered his great gift to society getting millions of young people hooked on reading. Haileybury has not forgotten him. Nor has Whitby or Sudbury, both in Ontario, where he penned several of the books in the Hardy Boys series.

As for the Mitchells, my fictional family, and others who survived the great fire, here's the rest of their story.

Harry and Amy Mitchell continued on with their newspaper work and soon had a new home for the *Haileyburian*. They both played a leading role in the reconstruction of the town, serving on several municipal committees and always proposing that the new Haileybury be even more beautiful than the old.

Max and Marty played hockey that winter on the temporary outdoor rink set up on the lake. Their skills improved dramatically. Max was named MVP of the four-team league and Marty won an award for his goaltending. Both young men excelled in the classroom.

Agnes Witherspoon's parents sent her away to a school in Switzerland to "learn some manners" and when she returned two years later she was offered a job as a public school teacher, working with J.H. McFarlane. She was devoted to her students and eventually married the assistant manager of the bank in Englehart—Cyril S. Baldwin.

The Dooley brothers served time in the penitentiary, having received two-year jail sentences. They returned to Haileybury upon their release and became known as two of the best pool players in the area. Sheriff Caldbeck visited the Dooleys in prison and told them about old Mrs. Lewis' strongbox. And how, when she passed away, it was found to contain over 30,000 dollars in cash. "Mrs. Lewis didn't believe in banking her money," he told the Dooleys with a laugh. "That's the one you passed on and should have taken, boys." Elmer Dooley shrugged and said, "Sheriff, I guess we weren't very good thieves—not like the Jamison boys. And we've learned our lesson."

Jesse Jamison and his cousin Bert, as repeat offenders, were each sentenced to ten years in the penitentiary. They never were seen again in the North Country.

Within a few months, Harry and Amy Mitchell made a momentous decision. With revenues from advertising dwindling because of the great fire, the *Haileyburian* was almost bankrupt. When Mr. Mitchell was given an opportunity to purchase a newspaper in the thriving mill town of Indian River, another northern community, and the bank approved his loan, he and his family reluctantly made the move. "Perhaps we'll come back some day," Harry and Amy told their many friends. "We love this community."

While Max and Sally were distressed over being separated, they recognized that the move was unavoidable and was in the Mitchell family's best interests. They promised to keep in touch through letters and phone calls and they vowed to visit each other whenever possible. But in time, contact between them became less frequent, they met new friends and eventually they drifted apart. But they would always feel a fondness for each other. And they would never forget how close they'd become on the night of the Great Fire in the north, and in the days that followed.

There would be no shortage of new adventures for the Mitchell brothers in the sports-minded community of Indian River, as you shall see in the second book in this series: *The Mitchell Brothers on the Hockey Highway*.